DESCEND AGAIN

DESCEND AGAIN

by

JANET BURROWAY

revised edition

introduced by the author

SANDNESS
MICHAEL WALMER
2022

This edition published 2022 by

Michael Walmer
North House
Melby
Sandness
Shetland ZE2 9PL

ISBN 978-0-6452440-2-1 paperback

*The publisher gratefully acknowledges the assistance of Robert Heatley
in the typesetting process for this volume*

INTRODUCTION

I remember the moment it seemed possible that I could write a novel. I was sitting in the bay window of my bedroom in the modest house my father had designed and built in Phoenix, Arizona. My desk was a repurposed vanity, all white enamel and jigsaw curves, topped with the portable Olympia typewriter that had been my high school graduation present. It was August 1956 and stifling under the drip-and-fan cooling system. I was home for the summer after my first year at Barnard College and would soon be heading back to New York and my repurposed life.

A few of my poems and stories had been published in *Seventeen* and the Barnard magazine *Focus,* and that had emboldened me, but maybe not enough for a whole book. I was thinking about, or making up, a woman of my mother's generation—distinctly not my mother. This woman would have grown up in a little town in southern Arizona that I knew about because I had distant relatives as well as a great-grandmother living there. I wanted to write about this woman mentoring a talented young Mexican student—which was itself a fantasy, because Mexican children were not taught in the all-white schools of that generation. Still, it was fiction, right? I had a clear image of the woman character. I could not quite see the boy. I sat trying to concentrate on him, but my mind drifted away from the page to something I needed from the dime store, and from there to trivial word play, and I was annoyed that my mind would meander in this way. All at once it occurred to me that Miguel's mind might be wandering in this same way, with the same annoyance. I started typing, at random but from his point of view, his thoughts full of food and puns and a punishing God. It was a clumsy attempt, but it felt like a *way in* to an imagined other. Later, whenever I wanted to get inside a mind unlike my own, I would try to find an image, a memory, a fear, a dream, a habit I shared with the character not-me. Then I would climb inside the imaginative wormhole and scribble out a few pages of that character in a *rant*.

I had, for reasons I have written about elsewhere, suffered the racial and class hypocrisy of my parents, my high school, and the Methodist Church. I was told that we all "believe in the Brotherhood of Man," but had come to find the claim hollow. What was so special about us for that? What was belief anyway, in that construct? I wanted to create, if not a world, then a small segment of one, that would mirror my anger, and my image of what could be. I set the book in 1942 and 1943, when I would have been six years old, and made my heroine a working teacher. The name of the town, *Sintiempo,* blatantly means "timeless," which I didn't intend as a compliment. I meant the town was fusty and entrenched, out of touch with the times. I was proud that the story would be completely invented, not a rehash of adolescent problems like most debut novels. Only many years later did I realize that both Millie and Miguel were straining against their circumstances and needed to get out of Sintiempo. Millie fails, and comes to terms with the place. Miguel succeeds. Many years later still, I realized that one of my methods in fiction is to trap my heroine in a situation I have found untenable, and then to get out myself.

Coming back to the book as it is to be republished, I was ashamed to see that, although Miguel's thoughts were in standard English, his dialogue was misspelled to indicate his accent. This was completely consistent with my upbringing—my mother taught elocution and was excellent at accents—but on the page it is racist, a literary sin I've preached against and could not let stand. Altering Miguel's dialogue to standard English is one of the very few changes I've made in the "revised" edition, since if I'd started improving, I couldn't have stopped. In particular I notice that Millie offers Miguel from her vast library not those books that would be most useful and appropriate, but those that I was encountering for the first time myself, by which I was enthralled. It turns out after all that I had more in common with Miguel than with Millie Delaney and her fabulous heritage.

Descend Again crept forward over the next three years, two at Barnard and then my first at Cambridge in England, in chunks, flashes, and frequent doldrums; between schoolwork, poems, short stories, a play. I was learning to write an English sentence, but in despair of a plot. I remember a day in the spring holiday from Cambridge, when I'd come to the south of France with friends André Schiffrin, Maria

Elena de La Iglesia, and Roger Donald (all would go into writing or publishing or both). We had rented, at two hundred dollars for the month, a big house on a cliff overlooking the Mediterranean. I was sitting in the courtyard with my Olivetti on the stone floor, struggling with some scene or other, and I whined, "What's the point of writing if it makes you *unhappy?*" The answer being, of course, that it will make you happy once you get it right.

It was that day or another that Leina demanded, in her you-hoo voice, "Ooh, put *me* in your novel!" I replied grandly that I would put her in *all* my novels! And I have. There are several Maria Elena de La Iglesias, Spanish and Latinx, in major and minor roles in Paris, Sonora, New Orleans and Georgia; a Mary Helen Church, and a "Lena Fromkirk" that Leina did not recognize as her namesake.

That summer I got a temp job at UNICEF in Paris and used my evenings and weekends finally to finish the novel. Because Charles Monteith at Faber and Faber had seen a short story of mine in the campus *Granta* and asked to see another, I sent him the fat typescript instead. When the letter of acceptance arrived I was so excited that I stumbled and fell on the stone kitchen floor of my Cambridge digs. But I was terrified that he also asked me to come in and talk about "a few editorial suggestions." I thought he would point out that the hero didn't live on the page, and I would have no idea what to do about it.

When I climbed the three flights of stairs to the disheveled cubbyhole on Russell Square, Charles Monteith—tall, portly, bald, and described by Hermione Lee in her biography of Tom Stoppard as "a mighty talent spotter"—sat me down and offered me a cup of tea. He said, in his plummy accent, "Miss Burroway, I don't think either of us is going to make a fortune, or indeed a living, out of this book." I was relieved; it meant he was willing to take a chance on me. But I didn't fully exhale until he suggested excising a few paragraphs here and there, and genially passed on to a publishing anecdote. Over the next fifteen years and four novels I would hear many such anecdotes; he was fabulous raconteur.

Descend Again begins with two convoluted sentences that betray how much Henry James I was reading that year:

The relative severity of what any society deems to be proper behaviour has no effect whatever on the rigour with which the members of that society uphold it. And it is not to be supposed that the idle rich are any more industrious about their prejudices than the indolent poor.

Once at a Faber cocktail party I was amazed to hear Monteith quoting this passage verbatim. My brother on the other hand, a newspaper editor in L.A., wrote that the sentence on the first page he liked best was "They sent her pies."

Over the next decades I tried to write more pies than Jamesian *mots*. Thirty-two years later I typed out that convoluted beginning as an epigraph for *Cutting Stone*, another novel set in Arizona, and ascribed it to "Juvenal," as in: juvenilia. So far no classical scholar has caught me out.

JANET BURROWAY

Chicago, April 2021

For

STAN

"... then we must not allow them the liberty
which they now enjoy."

"What is that?"

"The liberty," I said, "of staying there, and
refusing to descend again to the prisoners and
to share with them in toils and honours,
whether they be mean or exalted."

THE REPUBLIC, Book VII

Contents

Shadows

I

The relative severity of what any society deems to be proper behaviour has no effect whatever on the rigour with which the members of that society uphold it. And it is not to be supposed that the idle rich are any more industrious about their prejudices than the indolent poor. It is merely that in a town such as Sintiempo, which is without the leisure for post-deliberation on matters of propriety, what has once been settled upon as good enough is immediately declared to be the ideal solution.

For this reason, when Millie Delaney was orphaned at the age of thirteen and left alone in her father's house with an invalid step-great-grandmother of eighty-two, concern for her future had been briefly and charitably expressed. Then, as no one offered any further provision for her, the good people of Sintiempo thanked God that she had not been left entirely alone, and assured each other of their confidence in her pluck. They sent her pies. They seemed as unaware as Millie surely was that she was provided neither the freedom nor the guidance that parents are generally expected to bestow. She became both self-sufficient and quaint.

She was small, and as a child moved with a certain abruptness which never entirely left her, but which gained none the less a kind of grace from its becoming so wholly a part of her. This suddenness she spent in a perpetual arrangement of the old woman's comfort, an efficiency which verged on the officious; and when her efficiency left her long stretches of idleness, while the illness confined her still to the house, she read, because there were books, and there was nothing else.

The house was built on an Eastern plan, rather designed to exclude rain than to take advantage of Sintiempo's sun, and from the closeness of her continual reading Millie acquired a sense of unfamiliarity with the harsh hot weather, which most of Sintiempo did not share. The sun surprised her, and she squinted in it sometimes, which was none the less described, or thought of, as a lustre in her eyes. She was aware in a way that they were not of the differences and the likenesses between life indoors and out. Curiously, she was aware less often of recognizing in her reading a situation she had seen, than she was aware in Sintiempo of seeing a situation she had read. And she had not been for many years conscious of these comparisons before she learned to keep them to herself, expressing them only in a laugh as sudden as her gesture; a laugh which by virtue of its clarity and freedom conveyed that it found its victim charming. This single trait so endeared her in a region where charm was as scant as the rain, that they would have forgiven her almost any indiscretion.

Nowhere as in Sintiempo did good health so promote lassitude. The very foreignness of Millie's quick gesture, of her brow's sudden furrowing at the light, of her unexpected laugh, marked her distance from them even as it demanded their attention. In this, they often noticed, she was like her father. But indeed, they had long before attributed to her a likeness to her father in every aspect but size, and they had transferred their peculiar respect from him to her at the moment of his death in 1929, when Millie was not quite ten years old.

This respect, or more precisely, awe, had provided Milton Ellis Delaney with the perpetual benefit of the doubt; whatever unconventional he did was not imitated, but it was assumed that there was a reason for it. "Milton Delaney thinks big", was the general consensus, and this was sufficient to excuse whatever pettiness of character he might have shown.

His solid height had seemed to challenge that of the Lenajidak mountain, even as he had challenged the inaccessibility of its marble. He had generalized at a rate unknown to the members of that community, and when he spoke of the problems of the ranchers or cotton farmers or quarryers, he invariably substituted "the West" for "Sintiempo", implying a wider scope of comprehension. His neck was strongly and strangely formed, longer at the front than at the nape, so that his head was always tilted back as if his muscles were not sufficient to the weight of his brain, and so that his remarks went literally over the heads of his listeners whether they figuratively did so or not.

Nor was it only his bearing which gave rise to awe. He had after all come of his own accord from Springfield, Illinois, and horsebacked from Tucson to Sintiempo at a time when the town thought itself impervious to any economic or human innovation. He had cut a road into the forbidding ring of Lenajidak mountains, had hauled drilling equipment through this cut and set up the Lenajidak Marble Quarry, had mined the site for five years. He had at the end of that time had foresight enough to extract himself from the failing venture, found the bank in Sintiempo, and grow rich on it honestly. He had had the presence of mind to die the afternoon before the bank was closed in the great crash of 1929.

It was not merely success they admired in him, but grasp. Not that he forced a living out of the desert, which all of them some way or other did, but that he did it without reference to probability or concession to failure; that he died as he lived, with an infallible sense of the one right course of action. For this they forgave him a foreignness which itself acquired the authority of his actions; for a rich-voiced Baldwin upright which set their pianolas out of tune; for a delicate Italian table which mocked

5

their mountain; for a library of 2,500 tooled leather books which parodied the rough flourishes of their saddles; even for his one small wife, who had not, as Milton had, succumbed to the western accent, and remained herself therefore rather suspect.

Millie had been born when it was very nearly too late in both of the Delaneys' lives, and absorbing the calamity of the child's sex with the habitual calm of authority, Mr. Delaney christened her Milton Ellis anyway, though Sintiempo charitably forgot this, and never referred to her as anything but Millie or, on very formal occasions, Millie Ellie Delaney. When his daughter was seven Milton set about to import, like his piano and his table, her education. He sent for his grandfather's widow to act as tutor, but on the trip from Springfield the old lady had suffered an acute attack of asthma, and had shrivelled wheezing in the Delaney living room, from the moment of her arrival, while Millie went to public school. Milton gave his daughter his books, like his name, not because of any intrinsic worth they may have had, but because they were his own; and in 1929, as has been said, "of natural causes", he died.

The freedom thus awarded Mrs. Delaney, who had been considerably weakened since her daughter's birth, proved too much for her, and in 1932 she also died. Millie inherited the money under the technical guardianship of great-grandmother Geegee, learned to manage it, as she learned to manage the house, and read. That she wanted to go to college was as certain as that she could not, because of her obligation at home, consider it, and at nineteen she became a teacher of primary grades in the Sintiempo public school. In 1942, at twenty-three, she taught the single class comprising seventh and eighth grades, attended church occasionally, had coffee on Saturday mornings with Mrs. Angleberger, and read. She was popular with groups of young people, but with no one of them in particular, and aside from anonymous flirtations, no young man would have seriously considered himself the potential lover of so irregular a girl with so awesome a background and so wheezing a guardian.

"You know what's wrong with Millie Delaney?" Avril Hilton once observed irreverently. "Too much of her is on the inside."

II

Emitting a rich sigh from the vicinity of his third chin, Mr. Duncan Angleberger thrust a thick, deft forefinger between two slats of his picket fence and on to the back of a young June Bug. He tucked a thumb under the crisp belly and pulled it back through the pickets, waving it aloft.

"Geejune, hosephat! Now I gotja, baby. 'Ere we go, 'ere we go!"

He slipped a loop of red darning cotton over the shimmering head and drew the slip-knot tight. Sunlight glittered silver, gold and green from his glass rims, wedding band and the bright bug as he turned, cautiously unwinding the cotton reel. He let the beetle go. It fell headlong for a foot or more, righted itself with a click and whir, and flew till the thread was taut; then arched and dived, furiously circling him.

"'Ere we go, hup hup there!" Mr. Angleberger enthused, letting the line go slack. He twirled on the spot and squinted gleefully along the lifting string.

"June, Bug!" he sang. "Juh-uuunebuh-ug."

It was October. A feeble furnace blast of a breeze whirled at the half-mown lawn, scattering shorn clover and crabgrass along the walk. Mr. Angleberger drew first one squat leg and then the other to a stiff right angle and planted himself on the other side of the mower handle.

"Oh, hup," he laughed, and the sun beaconed forth his mirth in silver, gold and green glitters as he turned.

Mr. Angleberger was a man of mild deportment, and of whom the *Sintiempo Sun* was apt to speak in the passive voice: "Mr. Duncan Angleberger was to have been seen presiding this morning . . ." or, "Mr. Angleberger was reported to have selected . . ." But in spite of this journalistic insight, *The Sun* (which survived on Sintiempo's population by a careful rotation of local gossip, so that it gained a few customers as it lost a few) was never given cause to speak of Duncan Angleberger in other than his administrative capacity, and then never except to say, albeit in the passive voice, that the school system was running according to plan, that the text-books had arrived on time, that the convention had been attended as required.

They said of him in the town that he had never wavered from his academic ambition, and this much was true at least, that his superintendentship had been predicted for him as a boy, by teachers reasoning conversely from the fact that he was not much good at sports. Duncan had got used to hearing this dictum, and went without protest to take his administrative certificate at the university at Tucson. His basketball did not improve, and it was inferred that his scholarship was admirable. He returned to Sintiempo at twenty-one and married the most beautiful and frailest girl in town, for whose sake he had once as a child splinted the broken leg of a spine-toad. She died two months after, and six months after that Duncan became the superintendent of the Sintiempo Public School System.

The system was housed, kindergarten through high school, in one unadorned redbrick building. The faculty over which he presided never at any time exceeded six, and Duncan's job was as static as it was steadily performed. He had never made an innovation, nor ever vetoed that of a teacher, but he maintained order, and he was just. It was said of him also at certain times that his second wife had got the upper hand of him, but if this was so the influence did not encroach upon his job. It might have been expected that the intermittent fury to which he was subjected at home would have been, since he had no children, passed on to his pupils. But his authority affected him in another way; he used it as a harbour rather than a whipping stick. He listened to a defendant's version of a misdemeanour before he whipped, and he whipped without either malice or sentimental regret. On days when he beat a student, he made love to his wife. When he made love to his second wife, he woke thinking of his first. So whippings were infrequent, and their sting was not alleviated by the knowledge of injustice; they were greatly dreaded.

Mr. Angleberger now, circling, being circled by the beetle at the end of the string, pursed his mouth and conjugated tunefully, "Hosepho, hosephas, hosephat." Having so done, he inched sidewards toward the walk, rocking the darning spool on his open right hand and guiding the thread from his left fingers.

The beetle dipped and glided, droning monotonously as a distant row of schoolboys pledging allegiance to the flag. The horizon blurred behind him as his song blurred over the stillness, as if the same note could circle forever at the end of the string. So that when the screenhinge of the porch door screeched, Duncan started, and started again when the porch boards creaked and a stinging contralto voice called out, "You Who!"

The spool on his right hand hopped and rolled, slid perilously near the tips of his fingers. Duncan lunged after it like a juggler after a balanced broom, turning all the while, but the reel exceeded his grasp, poised for an instant on his knuckle and struck the cement with an insignificant sound. Over one shoulder Duncan watched it unroll lazily to the feet of the now descended Mrs. Angleberger. Mrs. Angleberger picked up the spool and reeled him in.

As he could not cease to pivot in his place without being bound by the circling bug, Duncan continued to turn, thus looping himself in the thread toward his determinedly winding wife. This considerably lessened the distance between them, so that as Duncan completed his fourth turn, one wing grazed Mrs. Angleberger's regal chin, which fell with a contralto shriek both terrified and accusing. With efficiency born of panic, Duncan snapped the string, and the June Bug retreated noisily, trailing a yard or so of crimped cotton.

Squinting, Duncan gazed after it as far as the sun's edge, and sighed from the diaphragm. Mrs. Angleberger tugged gently on the string. Duncan, his legs bound like barrel staves, hobbled around her so that Mrs. Angleberger, circling, being circled, completed the unwinding of Mr. Angleberger and the rewinding of the spool and placed the latter, with a gesture of possession, into a gingham pocket. Her unremarkable hazel eyes took on the colour of unmown grass.

"That's okeyduke now, Lena," Mr. Angleberger said in the tone of one forgiving an unhappy child. By this, through a series of associations with which each was intricately familiar, they understood that the Superintendent of the Sintiempo Public School System repented his truancy and the inconvenience caused to the tax-payer Mrs. Angleberger, and that after coffee he would sweep the walk and finish the grass. Lena's glint gave way to her everyday eye droop of patience, an expression which tugged also at the corners of her thin, downy mouth, and she too sighed.

Duncan preceded her blinking into the now dark-seeming living room. "Well, although," he said with defensive enthusiasm, "you know those tin wind-up crickets down the dime store?"

Mrs. Angleberger did not in fact know of these crickets, but as such an object was easy to imagine, she replied affirmatively, "Ummm?"

"Well, the toy business." Implying in his tone that the toy business was very good indeed. "Sintiempo you could bottle June Bugs nine months out of the living year. Sell them to the kids: Live June Bugs: String Included."

"We could make a fortune!" Mrs. Angleberger absently exclaimed, which was what she, always absently, always exclaimed at her husband's inventions, so that it would have been impossible to say how much hope, how much habit, and how much sarcasm the phrase contained.

Duncan, thinking of the liberated June Bug— where now?—chose to be disheartened. He grated a thumbnail against the grain of his chin stubble.

14

"Millie Delaney's due at ten fifteen, lordy, and the boy's not here with the cream," Lena said.

At Millie's name, Duncan perceptibly brightened, and letting the vision of the beetle fade from his mind, he rubbed a whole palm over the unmown chin. Then a thumb upwards along his upper lip, and he opened his mouth to speak, but:

"Better shave," Lena said first with considerable triumph.

"Heeby jeeby," mourned her husband bathroom-wards, pulling his shirt tail out by handfuls.

"Just one?" wasped his wife.

III

Gallencamp Emporium sat in the centre of Mesquite Street, so named for a row of haggard trees which sloughed their grey-green leaves, no bigger than raindrops, on its boardwalks. The leaves rotted in the crevices between the boards and made fertile slits for weeds which grew, were trampled down and grew again. They stretched in narrow furrows past Milton Delaney's Desert National Bank, The Silver Dollar Cinema, The Silver Dollar Saloon, Gallencamp's, the Rolled Gold Jeweller, Milady's Sun Fashions, and the Silver Dollar Five and Dime.

The Emporium was a clay box among these clay boxes, shielded from the October insistence of the sun by an awning which leaned slightly askew, striped in dying shades of green. A cracker barrel and a pickle barrel in which the crackers staled and the pickles turned rancid — but it was Gallencamp's one romantic notion of The Old West—flanked the open store front by counters of the week's new harvest from

16

Railton. A recently repainted script on the corrugated roof declared, "Gallencamp Emporium" in red and gold.

But inside, beyond the barrels, in the dank smell of vegetables there was little to merit such an elegant name. Not the rows of vacuum tins announcing flavours they concealed. Not the array of brushes, brooms, mops, dusters, scrubbers and scrapers steadily gathering dust. Not the mud-crusted lumps of Idaho potato tumbled in the bin. Least of all old Gallencamp's wizened hands, like rashers of overdone bacon as he scooped vegetables into a box.

"Two pounds carrots, twelve cents the pound, that'll be twenty-four."

"Carrots, twenty-four," repeated Miguel, inscribing the figure on a bill.

The errand boy stood scratching one ankle with the toe of his huaracha, and with his right hand pulled a nickel-silver bead chain in slow circles about his neck. A St. Christopher medal and a rabbit's foot slid heavily down the chain at each tug and clanked on the counter top. Gallencamp accorded him an occasional stern glance, not so much for the noise as for the left hand with which he wrote. Miguel was aware of the disapproval, and put his elbow into the flourish of every letter. He was the only left-handed Mexican in the Sintiempo Public Schools, and considered the fact of some significance. (Didn't it count for something? To be the only anything counts for something.)

"And a gammon roast, three pounds twelve, makes it two-thirty-nine."

"Two-thirty-nine," Miguel obediently mumbled. If Gallencamp himself, he thought, had seen a glory in the groceries, that might be something. But Gallencamp shovelled the golden carrots as if they were mere vegetables. He shunted the meats and the spices from the counter to the carton, tallied the account and shoved the load across to Miguel. Counter. Carton. Count. Cart. Watching him motionless Miguel dared to hum a few bars of, "As it was in the beginning, is now and ever shall be . . ."

"Miguel, boy! Fast hop, now; Anglebergers' first. I promised her by ten sharp."

"Yes, Mr. Gallencamp." Mumblingly. The protest of the barely audible assent. Miguel stooped, slid the box onto his left shoulder and shuffled rhythmically out into the sun . . . counter, carton, count, cart. Counter-cartoncountcart. Cartcartcartcart . . . The clap of his huarachas' heels stopped when he stepped off the boardwalk in front of the Silver Dollar Five and Dime, and he crossed the road in a heavier, dust-raising key. Shifting his load Miguel glanced back to the flapping awning. From this distance the sun spent some brilliance on the corrugated roof and the regal script. From this distance the Gallencamp Emporium might almost have been a theatre; it might have been the Silver Dollar Cinema with the screen rolled away for a recital or a skit. Three walls and a curtain, anyway, and the cracker barrel a kind of prop. If Gallencamp himself had seen it so.

Miguel shifted the carton back again to his left and slightly stronger shoulder, and walked on. The gammon roast, on the level of his nose, was beginning to leak through its wrapper and gave off a warm smell strangely like his own sweat. He wondered vaguely whether it were a sin to carry bacon to the Anglebergers, who were not Catholic, and were as likely as not to eat it on Friday and save their sole for Sunday lunch. And if it were a sin, whether it was a deadly— he was fairly sure that it was not—or venial, or carnal, or of omission. He had carried groceries to the Anglebergers every Saturday for two years now, sometimes without any fish at all, and had never referred the fact to his conscience. But he was thinking in terms of sin this morning, his mother having noticed the night before that he had added the rabbit foot to his St. Christopher medal. His mother was impressive in her loose white nightgown, her hair unwound and tumbling black to her knees. The very whine of her voice became resonance instead, and rolled like the voice of a prophetess around the close walls of their adobe house: "Miguel, the Lord he's going to punish you!"

He was rather inclined to disbelieve it. The Lord, he felt reasonably certain, would put the medal and the good luck charm in the same category, whatever it might be. But there was the fact that the rabbit had had to be killed for the latter; not to mention the pig which had by now entirely soaked its paper in grease. He sniffed it deeply and defiantly, resolving that he, Miguel, would eat ham any day he could get it, come what might on Judgement Day.

Yes, and then he would say, "Our Father who art in Heaven, I thought it was a filet of sole." Filet of soul. He laughed silently and hugged the gammon to his cheek. Judgement Day was a filet of soul, all sinners breaded and scorched, and pleading with watery eyes. Our Father, I thought it was . . .

But suppose God was more fierce than even his mother supposed. Suppose you had to make amends for everything you ate, pork and sole and rabbit alike. You would come before the Purgatory Emporium, and under an awning striped like the strings of a golden harp you would find all the animals you ever nibbled a flank of your whole life long. And then to get to heaven you would have to cast your pearls before the swine, kow-tow to the cows, wash the blood off the lambs, kiss the rabbits' feet. And what about the flies swatted up against your record? Explain that to God.

Gravely composing a poker face, without a break in his pace Miguel stepped aside and into the path of a red ant bearing a cotton-wood twig. He ended its efforts under his toe; dustpuffs rose around the slap of his shoe. He could feel the slightest pressure of the twig through the thinning soles (thin soul, Miguel enlarged on his pun; filet was better) but the ant he could not feel at all. So much the better. He did not look back. There, explain that to God.

He was passing the school grounds now, and the sun caught at the reflector of a floodlight above the baseball field. The face of God shone out at him from the reflector of a floodlight, blinding him, and the heavenly host was legioned below on the baseball bleachers, waving pennants and cheering Hallelujah! He squinted against the floodlight glare. Explain: on the morning of the 9th October 1942 you deliberately stepped on and destroyed . . .

Socorrerme. Sucker me. Now and at the hour of my ... Our Father who art in Heaven, listen to me!

He had passed the baseball field now, but walked on with hesitant steps, clutching the grocery box and averting his nose from the odour of raw smoked gammon.

Oh, God, I did not mean it. Do you understand the way you head goes winding down the street ahead of your feet? Your mind goes twisting up to Heaven, and your feet can't follow your head? And so they do something in the world . . .

Though Miguel had not the slightest doubt that he could win the softest, kindest shining of that floodlight God with his sincerity and his well-chosen words; still when Kep Hilton suddenly appeared around the corner of East Ocotillo and greeted him with a mumbled "Mor-rn", and a forefinger grazing the brim of his hat,

Miguel responded only with a grunt and a lift of his lip. He lidded his eyes down for the very brilliance of the thought in them. It was a bother the way your mind ran on. That's what he'd been meaning to say to God.

He hunched his shoulder to edge the carton away from his neck and turned into the street Mr. Hilton had turned out of. A sidewalk here. Countercartoncountcart. Cartcartcartcart. For instance, what do you suppose Kep Hilton saw along this street? Dirt, weeds, cactus, cats; if he saw anything at all. That's what you'd think anyway from his mumble and lunge. But what if everyone's hatbound head is filled with the vision of the brightness of the glory of the floodlit Lord?

He did not believe it. He stubbed at a sidewalk crack to emphasize that he did not believe it. Mud, grass, cactus, cats. A tom and a tabby were rolling in a zinnia bed, picking at each other's fleas or making love; he couldn't tell which. That stupid rhyme they were saying at school:

> *One dark day in the middle of the night*
> *Two dead cats began to fight.*
> *One had a mouse and the other had none,*
> *And that's the way the fight begun.*

Now aside from being stupid, that simply will not do. Either it's nonsense or it isn't, and if it's nonsense then sense has no place in it. It ought to go: One dark day in the bright of the night. But that doesn't sound quite right. Maybe, One dark day in the brilliant of the night. Shining. One dark day in the shining of the night, yes. Two dead cats began to fight. That part's all right. But the next line wouldn't do. If only one of them had a mouse, they might *actually* fight over that. It should be: One had a mouse and so had the other/And that's the way the fight . . . oh, oh. Mother, brother, smother, never mind. Stupid rhyme anyway. Ought to end: That's the way the fight began, but he'd filet his soul if he was going to correct their grammar. Wears you out to think about it. There's Miss Delaney.

Far enough away across the vacant lots that heat waves blurred and made shimmer a green green skirt, Millie Delaney came in the half-skipping way she had. At the top of his box Miguel had a loaf of raisin crunch for Mrs. Hilton, and though Gallencamp had said Anglebergers' first, he swung now into a driveway lined with rick-rack rows of brick. Mrs. Angleberger's reason for wishing him there at ten o'clock was Miguel's reason for wishing to arrive at ten-thirty. Why it was necessary to encounter Miss Delaney this morning he could not precisely have said. He did not plan to look up into her light-flooded face and confess that he had cold-bloodedly killed a red ant; nor for that matter to make any admissions regarding his taste for meat. Realizing with a sneer that he was comparing Miss Delaney to God, Miguel conjured the least attractive memory he had of her: the dark dress with the round white collar, the one that faded out against the blackboard, and Miss Delaney standing with a prim bright smile over the multiplication table.

He rapped on the Hilton back door and settled his carton on the porch railing. He heard a familiar Spanish lullaby, and the door swung back, complaining of great weariness. Señora Laureado's heavily-hair-wound face warmed to an equally weary smile. Jauntily Miguel responded by balancing the bread endwise on his head, a gesture the ridiculousness of which he was quite fully aware, but it pleased his mother, who shook a mop at him.

"Muchacho loco. Heesheeshee," she chortled, and winced sharply at some undesignated pain.

"You feel okay to be working?"

Señora Laureado rolled her eyes and nodded with effort. "Si, bueno," she lied, and then as Avril Hilton came up with a pan of hot cookies, she said in English, "Thank the Lord, he gives me the strength to work for Mrs. Hilton.

"It's Miguel with the bread," she added to Mrs. Hilton, beaming with tired pride. That Señora Laureado was really weary was as certain as it was certain that her only pleasure in life was a reputation for cheerful fortitude. She made the most of her considerable misfortune by garrulously making the least of it, in a perpetual commendation of her humble soul to God. Miguel did not love his mother, but he was painfully conscious of his debt to her—that is, the debt of his self, which he valued highly—and except in the presence of other adults he tried to be both respectful and pleasing. Señora Laureado, on the other hand, wholly loving her son, was never so much a mother as when she was being watched.

"Tsk," she worried now, "this box, it's too heavy for you to carry, Miguel."

"No, mamacita," Miguel shouldered the carton again and turned away. A beringed white hand detained him and familiarly pocketed two cookies in his shirt front. "Peanut butter," Mrs.

Hilton smiled as if her mouth were full of it, and added to Miguel's shudder of thanks, "He is shy."

"Don't spoil your lunch!" his mother called after him, and immediately began to hum the Spanish lullaby.

Miguel went quite a ways out of his path this time to turn a destructive toe on an ant bed. The possibility of his mother's suggestion, or rather of its opposite, intrigued him. If it were literally possible to spoil, that is to rot, instantaneously, on the spot, one's lunch, is it not possible that all mothers everywhere would abandon the phrase? Such, Miguel considered, is the logic of mothers.

Cartcartcart, he reached the sidewalk just in time to see the green of Miss Delaney's skirt disappear behind the Angleberger door screen.

At this sight Miguel perceptibly brightened, and crossing the road, he lowly intoned in a high voice the words to his mother's humming :

> *Soy, sola, sola,*
> *Soy sola y sin dueño,*
> *Solita sin amores*
> *Y en pueblo ajeño*

IV

Inside the bathroom, Duncan hooked his drab shirt over a dripping spigot and turned to the consoling luxury of his stone-topped sink. Abundance of surplus marble made opulent all the lavatories, coffee tables, hearths and kitchens of Sintiempo, but unfortunately this profusion of luxury cancelled out.

No, real consolation lay in the keenness of that consummately masculine instrument, the straight-edge razor. Firmly, with affection, Duncan lifted the whisker scythe from its dish and, clutching the strop on the wall, whetted with an appetite.

For Lena's limp shin whiskers, a slim Schick and one new blade per fortnight. And shaving dry, or with water and no soap; very very awkward. Very indiscreetly, Duncan considered, had woman presumed to the razing process. Very indiscreetly.

Now the thumb-on-blade test, the brush, the lather, the lathering, the poetics. Any man with a lethal edge at his Adam's apple being no mean pretender to the dramatic, and any man in a mirror being thereby bound to reflection, it is over the razor that he registers the advance of years, the retreat of hairs, the spread of the paunch, the shrivel of wattles.

Accordingly, "Heeby jeeby," commiserated Duncan for the sake of the advance, the retreat, the spread and the shrivel, and then, having thought of his wife's shins, he granted himself the poetic licence to continue considering them, a discouraging process of more poetry than licentiousness. Drawing downward on the bristle of one underjaw, he described to his superior beard, wordlessly, the inferior texture of the hair on Lena's legs (which, however, scratched surprisingly in bed). He was too honest, too just a man not to concede instantaneously the superior texture of her strawish blonde marcel to his own inferior shock, through which the finest comb displayed stripes of pate. His left fingers, testing, followed the razor over his cheek. Smooth and flawless, whereas Lena, under the powdering, bore the bitter scars of youth. She, poor girl, had aged before maturing, had felt the first track of crow's feet before she was rid of the adolescent acne. Her ears, now (the razor at his ear again) were fine, small, nearly flush with her face, not enough lobe to hang an earring on, but her teeth! Duncan showed himself a few of his own (which were normal and irregular) with a sideward stretch of his skin.

Big-boned Mrs. Angleberger had inherited from her father a shallow mouth and thin, straight lips, and from her mother, admirably large teeth. ("That," announced Dr. Abel Kregg, D.D.S., proudly but with some hint of envy as he extracted Lena's left lower back bicuspid, "is the largest tooth I have ever seen!") It had been a source of great embarrassment to her until she was well into womanhood that her aunts, and occasionally even her mother, would admonish, "Don't talk with your mouth full, Lena!" when her mouth was full only of teeth.

Mental reiteration of these facial dimensions occupied of Duncan's shaving time the plane of one cheek, and he extravagantly spent the other, the neck and chin on the delicate, less interesting (to us) proportions of his first wife.

If Karen Angleberger had survived the bare commencings of connubial bliss, perhaps Duncan's tenderness would not have. If Duncan's genuine mourning had not lasted such an unprecedently proper length of time, perhaps Lena Swope would not have been the only remaining single girl in Sintiempo. At any rate, Duncan's sorrow had worn thin with the irritation of widowerhood exactly as his bliss would, most probably, have worn thin with the irritation of a wife. The idea of Lena had wormed insistently into his mind like an idea of divorce, and presently he legalized a separation from solitude. And yet he retained one bittersweet vestige of better days. He would not yield the wedding ring his first wife had given him, and this was the golden thorn in the second Mrs. Angleberger's skin-thin side.

He showed the ring to his nearly shorn reflection now as, tauting his lip over his upper teeth like a toothless man talking, he neatly shaved his shadow of moustache.

From one or another of the foregoing remarks, it may erroneously be assumed that Duncan and Lena Angleberger were unhappily married. Quite the contrary. Wholly at home in her domestic patience and her domestic bizarrerie, Lena looked no further for content than the prompt arrival of the morning cream. Save for the velleity of a sunward buzzing bug, Duncan's heart set itself on no definable desire. After seventeen years, such a marriage may be included among the lasting things in life.

Lastly, a rinse and a brisk dry towel rub, and Duncan took up his shirt, which had before been damp, and had now been drenched from the spigot drip. It was, of course, then, necessary to have a clean one; a white one, why not; and a tie, why not. Back to the wall he went to his room so as not to be seen from the direction where now, in bird-soft soprano and shrill contralto, came the exchange of preliminary politesse. He put on the shirt, chose, in order to retain a certain nonchalance, a red string rodeo tie, and marched spiritedly parlourwards, tucking his shirt tail in by palmfuls.

"Thinner as ever," he greeted Millie Delaney with good-natured disapproval, thus allowing himself a thorough glance at her green-bound waist. Green as June bug; there's flying in that one, there is.

"Neither of us changes shape much, Duncan," Millie Delaney said, making room for him by swinging her bare feet from the couch and into the flat black slippers she had already shed. But he took a stiff-backed chair across the coffee table from her, reddening slightly in his already steam-pink face, and both he and Lena chuckled as if in appreciation of the subtlest wit.

Lena's laugh refined itself to a throaty aggressive cooing she habitually brought forth for children and social occasions, a sound which twanged slightly with the interference of her teeth. "Ooongc, she's looking a bit peaked," she agreed.

Millie took off her shoes again by stepping on the back of each with the opposite toe, tucked her feet under the green skirt, and confirmed Lena's remark with a smiling stifle of a yawn. "The first week of semester is always hard."

"Boys aren't giving you any trouble?" Duncan almost visibly shouldered the onus of his superintendentship.

"Oh, no, no." Millie accepted a cup of black coffee from Lena and shifted to make a mat for it a copy of the October *Reader's Digest*, which her hostess deftly rescued and replaced with a square of yellow marble.

"I'm sorry it's black, Millie, but lordy that boy from Gallencamp's hasn't got here yet. I swear I don't know what I'm going to do."

"You're going to serve black coffee," Millie suggested. "It's all right. It's an excuse for another cup when he comes." The grace with which Millie made rude remarks was a font of unending admiration for Lena, who risked neither rudeness nor grace. She sat back and crunched with an audible sigh into one of Avril Hilton's Thursday batch of peanut butter cookies.

"No, they don't give me any trouble," Millie turned back to Duncan. "They don't give me anything, not even a heartache worthy of the noun."

"Ooongc," Lena reacted automatically to heartache.

"The first couple of days they're absorbed in their new shoes and bookbags, about Wednesday they begin to realize the distance from October to May, the shoes get scuffed and somebody breaks a shoulder strap, and by Thursday they've hibernated; do not disturb until spring."

"Not showing up?" Duncan bristled with the fear of having to play truant officer.

"Oh, they come. Sleepwalking. It's partly my fault, but. . . ."

"Nonsense!" Lena said. "Have another cookie."

". . But it doesn't seem as if I ask so much. Some days I think if I could see one forehead wrinkling in good solid misunderstanding, I'd know what we were pulling them in off the ranches for."

"Have to get an education, Millie," Duncan remonstrated gently.

"I know. Yes, of course."

"Millie, sweetie, what's this about it being your fault. Lordy!"

"Don't really question the importance of your job, now?" The superintendent again, the handbook phrase.

"No, no."

"Well then!"

"You're just frazzled on edge, no wonder. Have another cookie, do. And, land, it's hard on them the first week, too, Millie, being cooped up out of the sunshine."

"I know."

"Hooo," Lena continued, describing small circles beside her ear with half a cookie, "you can't wonder at it, seeing them running over the fields in the summertime, chubby little legs after the horses, yellinnng," she rather yodelled the word herself. "Children are just naturally nature lovers, you know, lovers of nature. No doubt of it."

"No doubt of it," Duncan confirmed.

"Children," Millie said, "are the world's great materialists. The great 'natural' market for tin and plastic. The great 'natural' cult of Epicureans."

A small pause ensued while the Anglebergers tried to place the word Epicurean. Duncan had a vague notion that it had to do with cooking.

"They do like to eat," he ventured at last.

Not hearing this, and construing the strain as a sign that she had pressed their indulgence too far, "What I mean," Millie said more softly, "is that . . . we notice that they'd rather be outside than inside, and we attribute some glorious perception, some sixth sense to them because of it. It's not fair to them. We can't give them anything believing that. It's just that everything is new, and whatever is new is fascinating, like shoes and bookbags. If they'd rather live in the country than the city, it's not because they're . . . closer to God! It's because country things are better toys than city things. And even that's pure in a way we don't quite understand; uncluttered, somehow, accepting the world at face value. I mean, look at the connoisseurs of wine, look at the perfume sniffers and the soup tasters, look at the diamond merchants, people who spend their lives dealing in the learned, subtle differences and still never get away from things. Because in a way it is a higher perception, don't you see, not to be able to tell the difference between a diamond and a piece of broken glass. What is a diamond worth anyway, only some arbitrary 'refinement' of civilization makes it so? What difference does it make if it's lasted for a hundred thousand years? Except, part of what I mean is, that lasting does matter. And you don't discover that until you've lasted for a while yourself, and. . . ."

Even when incoherent, Millie was somewhat dazzling in the energy with which she tried to convince them of the cause of her listlessness. She was sitting on her heels and the short, rather too straight, rather too fine hair swung with restless emphasis as she talked. Ooohng, such grace, Lena thought. There's flying in that one, Duncan thought.

"...and things wear out," Millie said. "The face values fall through, even of fields and horses, and then you've got to have reasons for loving them, you have to have an idea or two to fall back on or you'll hibernate some winter and never come out of it but to die."

"Oooohn," Lena sympathized with death.

"Some of the boys in my class are fourteen years old! It's the last year of school for some of them. They've outlasted the newness, and I'll send them off to the quarry to mine marble to be sent away to be made into buildings they'll never have any desire to see and statues they wouldn't understand because I haven't begun to show them yet that ideas can make a thing precious or. . ." She was out of breath.

"There's Louellen Wesch," Lena suggested consolingly.

"Oh, Louellen learns her geography lesson."

"There's the new geography book," Duncan remembered. "Better, isn't it?"

"Bombo of the Congo. Yes, it's all right. It makes a story of it, at least; it does a better job than I do. Some of them will remember the circumference of the equator."

"Circumference of the equator," Lena mused curiously, "now I don't think I know what is the circumference of the equator," but Millie laughed sheepishly and shook her head.

"Twenty-four thousand, nine hundred and one point ninety-six miles," Duncan said, apologetic at having shown her up.

"So big as that!"

"And all of them," Millie continued, "will carry to their graves an image of illustration No. 22, the shiny black belly of Bombo of the Congo, who lives in a leaf but and goes elephant hunting with his daddy."

"What do you want, Millie?" Duncan was vaguely disturbed.

"I want . . . someone to want to go to the Congo."

"Millie!"

"What, sweetie? As a missionary?"

"No. Well then, I want someone to say, look here, how do you *know* the circumference of the equator is. . . ."

"Answer to that is simple arithmetic. And besides you don't know what the circumference of the equator is."

"No. Well, I want," she sat back and wrapped her arms around her knees, "another cup of coffee."

"Ooooh, I am sorry," but Lena was rather relieved than sorry. She whisked Millie's cup to the sideboard and repeated confidently, "you're just all tuckered, Millie."

"That's it, Millie. Tough tuckering work first week."

"And, Millie, baby, you're just wonderful with children."

"Absolutely, hunka dory." Duncan half reached forward to pat the hugged knees, but recovered himself in time and altered the gesture to a reach for sugar.

"You just love children, sweetie, you know you do."

"Absolutely," Millie agreed. "I'm not so hot as a nature lover myself." The slang phrase, which was Millie's ungrudged admission of defeat, had as always on her audience the success of the incongruous. Lena cackled and Duncan wheezed, such grace, there's flying in that one.

"Sorry about the cream."

A shuffling and a high humming beyond the back screen announced the grocery boy before his knock, and Lena set her green eyes for the second time that morning in a disciplinary glint. "Come in and about time. Set it on the sink and bring the cream to me."

Miguel brought the tune in with him as far as the sink and the settling of the grocery box, then dropped it and picked up the cream, making something of an entrance with the half-pint carton extended impudently on an open palm. Millie put her legs down and her shoes back on.

"Good morning, Miss Delaney," he greeted in model innocence.

"Good morning, Miguel."

"And into afternoon," Lena bristled. "Young man, did Mr. Gallencamp or did he not tell you ten o'clock."

"Yes, Mrs. Angleberger."

"And what does this clock say? You can tell time?" The latter question was asked not sarcastically but with sudden sincerity, and Miguel, blushing at her condescension, dropped his grin and his hand and answered, "Ten thirty-seven." Mumblingly. The protest of the barely audible assent.

Lena, indeed, the three of them, assumed the flush that dappled his high cheeks and flat nose to be a sign of repentance, and Lena softened somewhat, retreating to her twanging coo, "Ooongc, Miguel. Tsk, tsk, tch. Don't you know now you've made Miss Delaney wait for her coffee? Miss Delaney doesn't like that."

It did not escape Millie's notice that it did not escape Miguel's notice that she had the coffee cup in her hand, but neither of them protested. Duncan was alliterating his support, "Bad business, Boy."

"You'll not get on in this world that way, land no, Miguel. Why, hoooc, I shouldn't be surprised Miss Delaney would mark you down tardy in her book at school Monday, I shouldn't blame her the tiniest bit, isn't that right, Millie?"

"It's very important that you learn to be on time, Miguel," Millie said.

"Yes, Miss Delaney." Did she imagine the mocking note? Probably not, but a weak mocking. With his head down the shaggy lock of black hair covered his broad face from her view. He stuck his hands in his pockets.

"Well, run along now, and be early next time … here." Lena fished in her apron pocket and, as he turned, detained him to slip a nickel in his front shirt pocket. Doing so she crumbled two cookies, and withdrew her hand brushing it free of warm peanut butter while Miguel retreated wordlessly, letting the screen slam.

"And not so much as a thank-you," Lena said in an I-expected-as-much tone, lifting the cream spout and tipping it to Millie's cup. "Sorry about the carton, honey. I'll bet he's a trouble maker, that one."

"Doesn't seem to be, nope." Duncan searched a mental catalogue for offences.

"No, he hasn't the spirit to be a troublemaker," Millie said. "He's not even any lazier than the rest."

"Don't know about that," Duncan was still groping for a report of Miguel's character.

"Well, perhaps a little," conceded Millie. "You know something?" She darted her tongue about the rim of her mouth.

"No."

"What?"

"I think I like it better black."

Lena cooed and Duncan wheezed. Oh, that Millie Delaney. Barefoot for a third time Millie stretched and allowed herself a whole uncovered yawn and flung her arms over the back of the divan, asking, suddenly solemn, "Why . . . why is it very important that Miguel, what's his name, Laureado, learn to be on time."

"Well, why, 'll go up the quarry in a few years. Show up late there they'll boot him out. You know that. Where'd he be then? Hosephat, Millie, what's into you this morning?"

"Sorry, Duncan. The first week is always hard."

The quarry mentioned, talk turned as it always did in Sintiempo to the irony of the rich, unwanted mountain. Lenajidak hills had hidden until 1905 the four richest marble strains in America; a thick, shallowly covered core of white that faded on the western slope

43

into pale grey, and two deeper, slender veins of pink and yellow twisting under the northern valleys. In quality, Lenajidak's marble rivalled Italy's finest stone. In quantity, though not inexhaustible perhaps, it had not been appreciably depleted by the drilling of thirty-seven years. In hard cash, it was all but valueless. Italian marble came straight from the slopes of Carrara to the holds of American merchant ships, where it took free passage to New York as ballast, and it trundled at easy set rates from there to all main railroad junctions in the United States. Lenajidak was impassable to any vehicle but the horse and wagon, over a hill-stumbling steep road built by Milton Delaney in 1906 with more enthusiasm than engineering. It came in this primitive, perilous way all across the broad Lenajidak valley, through Sintiempo to the only exit in the spring-coil curve of the mountains, where it was hoisted from the wagons to the backs of flat-bed trucks. The trucks took the road outside the mountain ring, past the outside, impassable cliff of the quarry, two hundred feet below whatever insignificant hole had been made by the wrenching of the rocks on their backs, and veered on to Railton, completing an irregular circle and a half. At Railton the hooting Chieftan shouldered the load, which had to be reloaded to the Southern Pacific in Tucson for its California or Colorado market. The stages of the journey were carried out with a clockwork insensibility, no hand knowing what the others were doing, caring less. But the regularity and efficiency of the home market did not prevent the fact that, even on the west coast, Italian marble was cheaper by some 20 per cent than marble from Lenajidak. Consequently, Sintiempo took the complicated job of catering to out-of-the-way Southwestern markets, and as the demand for top-grade marble was not at its peak either in the mid-twentieth century or in the American rural Southwest, the Lenajidak Company dwindled at a much greater rate than the Lenajidak peak.

Nonetheless, the venture had not been valueless to Sintiempo. It had brought an initial influx of eastern money that had found its way into the valley cattle ranches and cotton crops, if never back to Wall Street; it had brought a settlement of cheap Mexican labour which, shacked on the southern foothills, remained cheap if not laborious; it had brought a brief notoriety in the geological journals which still sat in modest stacks on bookshelves otherwise bare but for the bible, in perhaps a dozen Sintiempo homes; it had brought Milton Delaney.

"Ooo, lordy Millie, if your daddy was alive he'd get them a new road in there," Lena averred nostalgically, though in fact Milton had dropped all but his banker's disinterested interest in the quarry as soon as the bank itself was sound.

"No doubt of it," Duncan said again, who found it expedient to echo thus his wife's most doubtful statements.

"It wouldn't pay for itself," Millie shrugged.

"Good money after bad," Duncan hastily confirmed.

They spoke of the quarry with mild futility, like people who attend a funeral out of social duty, and it was exactly this tone that the mountain's rich, scarred face mocked. Nearly everyone in Sintiempo had some small nest egg scrambling in the quarry account books, but hardly anyone except the labourers depended on its balance for a livelihood, and the salaries were small enough to be assured. Like all prophets and saviours, Milton Delaney had stormed into solid stone, created his world there, and retreated leaving a functioning ghost town. Lena wondered idly about the height of Lenajidak.

"I mean, do you suppose like a thousand feet, or what now?"

Duncan knew the exact figure, and this led them, admiring him, back to the circumference of the equator, the new geography book, the brightness of chubby little Louellen Wesch. Millie thought she had better go.

"Oooh, just one more cup, have a half Millie."

" 'Nother cookie, Millie, you'll waste away."

"No, really," she hooked a finger in a shoe to straighten the back of it, stood and stretched again. "Really, there's so much to do at home. Geegee will be wanting her lunch, and I've got to go over Monday's lessons. A summer off makes me creaky on my arithmetic."

Lena chortled and Duncan wheezed; they showed her as far as the porch and gazed after her as far as the gate's swinging. The gate latch trapped a green hem corner, and Millie jerked it free with an impatient motion, swung round to wave, and went in that half skipping lift of a way she had. Duncan, enlightened by her revelation of the materialist souls of children, was reflecting that perhaps live June Bugs were no competition on the toy market for tin wind-up crickets. Lena was wondering what, if any, effect a green sash wrapped that way several times around would have on her waistline. So that Duncan rather startled her by the decisive tone of his, "Nope, probably wouldn't work."

"What?"

"Bottling June Bugs."

"Change," Lena enunciated, "your shirt before you finish the lawn."

Duncan complied without so much as the distortion of an epithet.

V

Milton Delaney had built his house a moderately inconvenient distance from Sintiempo proper, after a city notion (which immediately became Sintiempo's) that the socially superior take to geographic isolation. He had built it moreover with its face to the mountain and its back to the town, so that now across the bare lots Millie headed toward a screened kitchen door and gold chintzed windows in a bulk of mustard stucco, surrounded by spare pyracantha bushes and lean stalks of yellow yucca.

She walked more slowly as she neared it, swinging her arms and feeling the sun bake at her forearms, bare under folded shirtsleeves. To be ugly and therefore misunderstood, to be hated for a wart at the end of one's nose or a stammer in one's speech or an unfortunate turn of phrase, lends to the inept, the stammering and the bewarted a dignity of martyrdom that was denied to Millie Delaney. Insensitive hatred leaves the soul in its own good company, but insensitive adulation bandied Millie between trifling high spirits and a lonely sense of deception. She had never failed herself by imitating the local fad or the current view, which failing her very reputation forbade, but without willing it she became the reflection of her effect; was demure with those who praised her modesty, gay with those who responded to her life, vague when she was credited with profundity, charming as a guest, prim as a school teacher, officious as the nurse of an invalid.

And if therefore she whipped her green hem from the gate latch and waved with a joy of something very like good fellowship, by the time she left the road for the dustless heat of the veined ground, she was heavily hollow, and reflecting again that the first week of semester is always hard. Here, a mound below a crooked mesquite tree was scarred with the charcoal of old bonfires and spattered with broken bits of whisky bottles, gold and brown and green. By squinting through lowered lashes Millie made the colours spread and merge, the glass gravel flinging light as a church window seen through a heavy veil. It was such a vision as a child might see, taking the world at face value, accepting any stained glass as a work of art, and it served in some measure as a confirmation of what Millie had tried to say to Anglebergers, and they had not confirmed by understanding. She stooped and swept from a ragged tuft of grass the dark stub of a beer bottle bearing the words "no depos". Who might it be? Degradation to the temperance society, slovenliness to the community clean up committee, danger to an anxious mother; or a hunk of uncut amber, the mild iris of an enormous cow, of the grocery boy in his blank dark gaze. Acknowledging that this was further even than her imagination cared to go, she stretched on tiptoe and flung the jagged glass in air, where it somersaulted in a glimmering arc, the head of a flung tomahawk, thunking against and gashing the bark of a palm tree.

The palms lined the road she had left for a ways, but were older than the road, so that the road detoured to match their gently irregular path. They extended in the slender, tough growth of a hundred years, fanning their fronds suddenly at the summit, and they were Millie's first memory.

She was three, it was Sunday, and she wore a taffeta dress with a ruffle that swished against the kneecaps of her white silk stockings. She still had the dress somewhere, and particularly remembered the colour of it, which was called wine-colour, because in no other context had she heard her mother use the word "wine" with approval. Her mother had been in the upstairs bedroom, twining the wisps that escaped from her dark pompadour into tight shining ringlets around the blade of a curling iron. Milton said, "We'll take a little walk, there's plenty of time, Maud," and so clutching her offering envelope in the ruffled pocket of her dress with one hand, and her father's hand with the other, she had walked with him a way down the road, lifting her knees and setting her soles flat, careful of scuffing the patent leather. From a distance the palms were insignificant enough, but when they stood beneath them and her father leaned his head back staring up, she did the same, and saw the enormous height of Milton Delaney, his grey hair splaying and drifting gently in the wind, dwarfed by the enormous height of the tree, its fronds splaying and drifting gently in the wind. She was doubly struck, complexly for a child of three, with the fact that her father was not the tallest thing in the world, and with the fact that she had always assumed that he was. The head of the palm beneath which they stood tilted slightly in a stronger drift, and she suddenly saw it stare beyond to another child in a wine-coloured taffeta dress, as much taller than the tree as her father was taller than she. And beyond that a grey-haired man as much taller than the child as the tree was taller than her father. And beyond that a tree, a child, a man, a tree in stiff military row; a taffeta dress, a fan of grey hair, a fan of green frond, a ruffle of wine-coloured hem, on into the sky, to the top of the sky, and just as the blowing spikes of a frond were to scratch the ceiling of heaven it receded and drew away, making room for a child, a man, a tree. As many times as she spent seconds staring this happened again, that heaven was to crack, and drew away, and the children and the men and the trees kept multiplying, growing, until her father, now grossly small, tugged at her hand, compressed his lips and raised his eyebrows to express his appreciation, and she, dazzled and choked, could reveal of what she had seen, only the broken word, "Ta-all." Milton nodded, as if she had expressed his sentiments exactly, but Millie somehow knew that he had seen nothing but the tree.

From her fourth and fifth years she held vague, fond memories of corrugated building blocks, the pattern of the kitchen linoleum, the smell of her dainty mother's dresses under the sleeve. But nothing for many years came back to her with the force and frequency of these heaven-splitting palms, and the word, and the idea, of "tall". The idea was precious because she could not express it, almost as if she had not yet learned to talk, and when she learned to write she tried to put it on paper, but beginning with the word 'tall', she could get no further, and retraced the letters with a heavy pencil until they ran blackly into each other and she had turned the T into a squat, clumsy palm. Later something else, a polliwog when she had discovered the first sprout of its frog's legs, had impressed her as a moment of extreme significance, which it was her duty not to forget, and she determined to make a mental diary, retracing only in her mind, and counting on the tips of her fingers, the moments whose mattering she must remember because they would matter to no one but herself. But then, though she tried to make her selections judiciously, she began to watch for the moments, settled once for a party at which she won the egg-hunt, once for a sunset which was praised by her parents beyond her own appreciation of it, once for a pony her father gave her on her eighth birthday. Though she had kept, and kept secret, this list for many years, as she matured the memories from the ring finger on her right hand to the thumb of her left paled and became childish, dated like a bad book. But the palm trees on her right little finger recalled always a sky blowing and extending in swaying rows of wine and grey and green, ruffle and lock and frond.

Millie lifted to her toe tips as she passed the last tree which, like herself, was twenty years taller than her first memory of it, and raised her arms in a reaching or a greeting. She felt as she did so a flicker of unreasoning promise, though the next moment, stepping down into the flagstone patio of Milton Delaney's house, she imagined herself rousing her class from its indolent indignance and Bombo of the Congo, bringing them here, and she knew that she would be able to impart to them no appreciable knowledge of palm trees but the broken word, "Ta-all". And that they, nodding in conventional classroom assent, would perhaps see nothing but the tree.

She threaded between the spindly yuccas—"Thinner as ever," she greeted them under her breath—and breaking a pyracantha branch for the mantelpiece, looked back to the hot dry town, scattered like the charcoal debris of old bonfires over the pit of the valley. She unlatched the screen and the chintz-hung door, and was met by a new heat, no different in degree, but smelling of human age and cooking fat, and hung with the sounds of a creaking chair and a faint harmonica monotone.

"IT'S ME GEEGEE," she shouted in no particular direction, and was answered irrelevantly, "Home, are you then?"

To which Millie, slicing the pyracantha branch with a butcher knife worn to half its width, irrelevantly and quietly replied "Yes I'm home then," and tossed the knife into the stained marble sink.

A man in a southern voice and an eastern skin cut westward over the border from northern New Mexico. He rode somewhat unsurely a not-too-surefooted Pinto mare purchased from a Houston dude ranch at no gift of a price. The nag, no doubt sensing this, bared her yellow teeth and showed the recesses of her well-worn mouth with every step's slack of the bridle. Her rider of something less than thirty years was humming, "When Those Cassons Come Rolling Along". He did not, however, realize that he was doing this, and if he had, he would not have been.

There was no marking of the border at this point in the roadless dunes, and he crossed into Arizona without knowing it, feeling in fact that he must surely have done so some twenty hours before. He had more or less lost track of the date and there was nothing in the landscape, thick round boulders of red rock on sand hills almost blue in the early light, abrupt spikes of stiff cactus and straggly mesquite, to suggest that it was October, but of this much at least he was fairly sure. Neither did he wear a watch, but it was an hour of dawn he knew with more precision than the hands on a clock face disclose. With one hand on the rein, and the heels of his Cordovan shoes knocking loosely against the rib-marked flanks, he fished with the other fingers into a pale blue pocket, withdrew a muslin pouch, and working the string with his teeth, rolled a cigarette without using the hand on the rein. He scratched a match on a tin stud near the saddle horn, and smoked with an awkwardness that was evidently habit and not inexperience, holding the cigarette to the left side of his lips between his right fingers, so that his palm covered his mouth and his thumb lay along the side of his nose.

"And where'er you go, you will always know..." he hummed through his lips, his fingers and the smoke, slapping the rein in absent time to the tune and the steady plodding. He was with enjoyment falling behind in a daily race he ran from the early hours with the chasing, rising sun. He had started dark, and rode ahead of the morning west, feeling the glow gain constant ground on him. It was the only game he knew whose satisfaction lay in the losing. The sun tagged him now on a muscular shoulder nonetheless somewhat stiff from unaccustomed sleeping on a saddle of a pillow, and acknowledging his defeat, he reined in the all too willing mare, squinted the sun full in the face and toasted it from a canteen.

He was a white man, and particularly so; hair no colour of known blond, but moon-hued on a head too carefully, finely formed for the height and power of his body; skin as smooth and taut as milk glass, and yet not now an indoors pale; sun burned white, as if to touch it would sear the hand.

Not all running men are hunted, and if Karl Ormerod of the Houston Ormerods had known the truth from which by choice he now isolated himself, the two authorities he fled were relatively unconcerned, and had given up all but the technical position of pursuit. As far as he knew he was a double desperado of the New West, fleeing the uniform and the bars. But the bars fronted the teller's window of his father's bank in Houston, before which he had taken a temporary stand under guise of settling down. The uniform was khaki.

"I don't believe in war," sullenly he had said, and the recruiter, so mild a man himself that he wished to skirt even the smallest skirmish with this warful youngster, had wearily suggested, "A conscientious objector?"

"Just an objector," naïvely Karl of the Houston Ormerods had said.

From no small distance in the clear desert heat could one have seen enough to guess that Karl Ormerod was an able-bodied man. A-1 was the way the government worded it. As a consequence of which, since as a matter of modest fact he conscientiously did not believe in war, he was now two weeks on the way from Houston, and over the Arizona border just about dawn on the 9th of October, 1942.

An unexpected chilling draught slid whistling from the higher ground ahead, and in ungrudged acquiescence Karl mounted and climbed around behind a bouldered hill, dodging its path. It was a way he had of treating the weather, which men like his father and Milton Delaney do not understand; he preferred a sky clear not for the comfort of it, but for the simplicity; and if he knew enough to come in out of the rain, he did not know enough to resent his having to do so. He liked this country for its barrenness, for the steady predictable rise and fall, and would have liked it better without its stubborn cactus growth and occasional oasis; he was not afraid of the snakes and gila monsters or the slim lizards that sometimes whipped like living twigs from beneath the hooves' intended path, but he could have done happily without them, for their suggestion of something under the skin of this otherwise undeceptive land.

It must not be inferred from this that Karl was indifferent to life, or to the lean and low and mud-coloured forms of it. The lizard he thought a misplaced city beast, and would have welcomed here the arid simplicity of a Houston tramp, who kept his colours regardless of his background, and made his demand concisely clear. It is hard to know what a lizard wants. Where the others were concerned, Karl was a giver of alms, and not with the tooth-pursed, purse-mouthed christian grudge of the Sintiempo almstraders of the world; but a giver of alms as if whatever his pocket held was known by no name but alms. He might have spread his final fifty cents on his open palm, have halved it with the supplicating sot, and solemnly said, without irony: "Now damn it, that's all you get. I've got as much right to it as you have." He would, they were saying in Houston, come to no good.

He was coming at any rate rather suddenly over the stubbly dune to a fairly good-sized town. A forlorn and distant wail wound toward him from the direction of his own approach, and he realized that he had been for some time travelling beside and out of sight of the railroad track. As abruptly, he ran perpendicularly into an asphalt road, and turned on to it behind a flatbed truck, which swayed under blocks of rough cut marble. At this sight he dug his city heels into the mare, who was not in the least affected by his prod, and rode forward to the town in the attitude of a gallop and at the pace of a trot.

He crossed the track behind the truck and ahead of the train, and watching the former pull with a groan of gears into the railroad yard, passed on into Railton, which was blinking its windows and unfolding its awnings onto a new market day.

A man in comparative repose, a man like a Chihuahua dog, langorous blue eyelids and erect pointed ears, wearing a black shirt and a black moustache and an elegant buckle of Zuni Turquoise, leaned on the side of a lettuce shed smoking a black cigar and issuing an occasional order to the boys who trotted lettuce crates back and forth without perceptible plan.

He watched Karl's approach in silence, taking in both the pallor and the strength of his arms, and said nothing until Karl had dismounted and come forward with the courteous inclination of his head that he had acquired against his will in his father's bank.

"Morning."

"Morning," affirmed the man in comparative repose. "I wonder if you could help me."

The man like a Chihuahua dog ventured no opinion on this matter, but made no particularly discouraging motion, and Karl proceeded, "I'm after a place called Sintiempo."

"You're practically before it," said the man with the langorous blue eyelids, without waiting to finish his joke before he began to laugh at it; a round high howl of a laugh which continued for several seconds. It faded off while Karl stood waiting with a polite curl of his upper lip.

"Twenty, twenty-two miles south as the crow, as they say."

"I don't need a road," Karl said indicating the horse, which was drooping its neck in apparent contemplation of his Cordovan heels. The man with the pointed ears too looked at Karl's shoes, and in a tone both confident and confidential warned.

"You'll need a road a'right, or a better nag than that, m'boy, and both, most like. You can thumb a truck if you wait till lunch, but what for, I wonder; what for, if my asking isn't too…"

"No, no, not at all, sir. I'm looking for work in the quarry there. I understand. . . ."

"Nope," said the man in the black shirt. The word, which was intended as astonishment, came out like a bald refusal.

"What for, I wonder," wondered the man again.

"I understand they're short of hands."

"No doubt, no doubt of it, and no wonder. It'd take you a year on that horse, my boy, circling the whole damn mountain ring before you c'd find your way into it."

"Are the mountains rugged?"

The man with the black moustache bit at it and rolled his eyes. "Like a fortress, m'boy. Like a stone teacup. Like the White Cliffs of Dover." As neither Karl nor the man had ever seen the White Cliffs of Dover this image carried considerable strength.

"Just what I'm after," Karl said.

"Nope," again, and this time the tone was clear. "Not at all. What for, I ask you? Heavy labour and a light wallet and shacking with wetbacks, pork and beans. Not a job a man would hunt for, not at all."

"Thanks, though," Karl turned away, but the man hooked one thumb in his Zuni buckle and the other in the crook of Karl's arm.

"Now you have the look," he said, "of a man who knows a little arithmetic." Karl was not aware that it showed, and said as much, to which the man with the black cigar performed his amiable howl, emitting hoots of heavy smoke.

"Now I am in a position," he said, straightening his spine to indicate the uprightness of his position, "to offer you a temporary job as a clerk-accountant in the Smee Lettuce Packing Company, at twenty dollars a week and board. My wife is a mean woman with a barbecue pit," he added.

"I was heading for Sintiempo."

"But what for? End of the world itself, that place is. Won't get your mail three times a week, won't hear the news of the world till it's three weeks past your caring."

"That's what I'm looking for. But thanks."

"I appeal to you," the man said with sudden earnestness, grinding a tooled boot toe on the black cigar. "I've a record season's crop in the stacking and bookwork up to the chin. My secretary is gone chasing a mestizo trucker half-way to Canada and I can't leave the sheds myself for fear they'll leave the stuff rot here and send an empty boxcar to the coast. Hey boy!" He yelled at an Indian youth heaving a crate to the back of a truck. The boy came carrying the crate, and the man scowled a sorrowful canine scowl. "Look here. You see the red stamp; that means Sante Fe. You send that head to California it'll be dead withered before it hits the border." The boy retreated sullenly in the opposite direction. "I appeal to you; do you see what I mean?"

"I do," said Karl, "but. . . ."

"It's indoors work," the man pursued in blatant deference to Karl's white skin, "and forty hours, and an adding machine."

"You're really stuck are you?"

"Ham-strung. Tied. Absolutely. My name is Vernon Smee." He offered an open hand, and as Karl hesitated, added kindly, "any name will do, m'boy."

Karl shook it. "Oliver Karlton," he said.

"Oliver give us a try."

"It's not as if I was in a hurry, after all. I'll give it a month," he said.

He gave it, in fact, eight, delaying his objective until the Smee Lettuce Packing Co. was tidied for the year into columns of his round and childish hand.

VII

Seasons in Sintiempo cannot be seen. There is no snow. The sands shift in the same drifts of burning pallor every noon, the blinding face of the marble mountain in Lenajidak quarry grows steadily with each day's drilling, the cottonwood trees burst their bolls in early summer and heap the porches with a snow of warm thistles. The rain comes at its own convenience headlong into the ground; the cacti swell and the sands lie still for a day. Roses bloom between October and April, prickly pear and Saguaro in June, sunflowers and hollyhocks all year round. When a tree sheds its leaves, they cut it down.

December is least subtle of the months, but the cold is frostless, bitter dry, like hate expressed in the most formal terms. On December evenings Millie used to sit on the floor by the fire grading papers, aware of and accustomed to the pewter-coloured eyes that measured every move.

"Comfortable, Geegee?" she would ask occasionally. The old woman was deaf, and whether she read lips was never altogether certain. Certain it was that no action in the room escaped her. She sat rocking wrapped to the elbows in a multi-coloured afghan, consuming the view with flat grey eyes that seemed to Millie almost, at times, concave, like the bowls of pewter spoons. She sat and observed, mutely digested her observations, and when she felt she had been spoken to, wheezed forth her distillation of the world's great truths.

"You'll catch your death on the floor, Millie."

This Millie acknowledged with a solemn, absent nod. "Would you like to come closer to the fire?"

In reply, Geegee took from the round marble table beside her the over-sized harmonica that was, by choice, her only diversion. She played it feebly and monotonously, slipping in and out of the half dozen tunes she knew in unintelligible medley. To this accompaniment, both plaintive and mocking, Millie corrected the spelling errors of the twelve and thirteen year olds of Sintiempo. The results seldom varied: Louellen Wesch, 8o per cent; Larry Hempstead, illegible; Ann Gallencamp, meticulously lettered total error; Morena Garcia, fifteen attempts, fifteen erasures; Miguel Laureado, four words sprawlingly correct, otherwise blank; Harold Tso, mistakes identical with those of Louellen

Wesch; Doreen Sammon, one small doodle of a disproportionate horse.

She laid aside the papers and poked the fire. Above the mantelpiece a mirror extended to the ceiling, and Millie briefly searched her face for lines. There was only the black hair falling, not beautiful but soft, around her face; slight bones; a nose as gently beaked as a small bird's beak, and no less appropriate. Ugly nose, she observed to herself without conviction. With a pencil suspended on a red silk cord, she drew a line through the date. The calendar hung between mantel and bookcase, a trio of dour, rapt Magi against an incarnadine sunset, an unpunctuated roman script MERRY CHRISTMAS GALLENCAMP EMPORIUM, and unassumingly below, the numbers of the days and year.

If the season, the month and the holiday were to be seen most clearly here and not in the streets, the same was true of the year. The twentieth century had penetrated Sintiempo, but only in the most superficial and arbitrary ways. The calendar, for one, declared it; the newspaper inevitably suggested it; the radio insisted on it, and in fact no fewer than twelve Sintiempo youths had joined "our boys overseas". But these were local losses, like the loss of a cotton crop, and Milton Delaney, who thought big and might have been able to lend them some wider significance, was dead. And so Sintiempo's acknowledgement of the world situation consisted primarily in the purchase of small green stamps and the knitting of multi-coloured afghans.

There was food rationing in Sintiempo, but Gallencamp was not one to haggle over the precision of his inventory. The town was rich in cattle, and if the allotted beef supply ran short, who was to say from what cause a dozen of the B-Bar Ranch best steer had died? The Mexican village would go gratefully short of sugar for a price-cut on wine; the chickens did not stop sitting for the sake of a foreign blitz. So that as long as the monthly account at Gallencamp's was regularly paid, the ration coupons could come as they came, and Mrs. Gallencamp would receive them with a pleasant remark on the weather, and without looking at her palm.

There were automobiles in Sintiempo, but the automobile was of no practical value; it could not herd cattle, it could not pick cotton, and it could not get up the mountain to the quarry. To be sure, it enabled some experience of the world beyond, and without it perhaps no one would have known that there were escalators in Los Angeles and public bathing beaches at the Great Salt Lake, but the reminiscences of Sintiempo vacationers yielded little of greater urgency. There were still more horseshoes sold in the town than tyres.

There was a library, so financially neglected that its main source was the discard bin of the county seat Carnegie. The volunteer librarian bought watery romantic novels which, however, went unread, and religious publishing house pamphlets on the Biblical Problems of the Modern Christian. The latter were surprisingly in demand—and yet not so surprising perhaps in a town where Shakespeare was quoted unintentionally if at all, and the Bible itself told about, looked at, referred to, carried around, and sworn upon without necessarily ever being read. It was a library not quite so large, quite so complete, nor quite so generally disregarded as the library in Millie's living room.

Milton Delaney had inherited his books by default, being the only one of the Springfield Delaneys not to express himself on the subject of their possession in a definite negative. It had been the varied but not impulsively selected library of a great uncle, a professor of classics at an Illinois university. It contained no watery romantic novels or biblical pamphlets of any era, and Millie was left with the unshakable impression that philosophy and letters had disintegrated at the turn of the century. That this could not be true she knew well enough, but of evidence to contradict it she was offered none. And having in her private possession a cornucopia of thought that she could not in a lifetime exhaust or tire of, she did not look very far.

For these reasons, and because she was more strictly than anyone confined to Sintiempo, Millie was most at home with authors farthest from her own time, and peculiarly at ease in the abstract. Though she was fond of Dickens, Tolstoi's people seemed to her more colour-fill. Lucretius' universe was clearer than the world Wilde had constructed of minute details for which she had no model. London and Paris she conceived childishly, vaguely, but the *Republic of Plato* was inflexibly clear.

It was to that book she moved now, hesitating once as her hand strayed over her own name in gilt on the leather spine of *Paradise Lost*. No, not Milton in winter, she decided, and reached beyond for *The Republic*. The harmonica stopped long enough for Geegee's admonition, "Always reading, always working. All work and no play."

"Holidays soon," Millie assured her irrelevantly, pointing to the calendar, and the old woman, comprehending, complained "Christmas", before she took up the wandering tune again.

Millie held the book, a small volume, flat between her hands for a moment, and then let it fall open of its own accord at the metaphor of the cave. By force of the same habit Millie's eye fell to the third line:

> *Picture men in an underground cave dwelling with a long entrance reaching up towards the light along the whole width of the cave; in this they lie from childhood, their legs and necks in chains. . . .*

Oh, it was a game she should have outgrown, she knew. Plato had not meant to write a parable of her own dissatisfaction, her own hope. And yet . . . the heavy darkness of the room, the pebbled grey of wallpaper, the creak of the old woman's chain, her chair. And promised in her books, her mind; in herself but beyond the rock walls of Lenajidak, who could say what light there might be the whole width of the world?

With a finger in the place she crossed again to the mantel and sat before it. The light dappled over the page. She skimmed the words because she could supply them.

From old habit, and with a kind of satisfaction too young, too energetic to be called morbid, Millie looked up from the book to her shadow, and the shadow of the rocking woman on the opposite wall. The silhouette rocked, a metronome to the insistent, assonant rasp of song.

Racing over the words she read the life of the philosopher, dragged from the darkness, blinded by the sun, embracing the light, hurled a martyr to the cave again to be cursed by the slaves he has come to free. More concretely than any named, imprisoned hero she saw him strain to live alone in the sun, and denied the liberty...

Arbitrarily, mid-phrase the harmonica stopped, and Geegee leaned laboriously forward in the chair, "Millie?"

"Millie! Move away from there and come under the lamp. You'll ruin your eyes."

Reflections

VIII

" 'Descend.'"

" 'Descend.' Umm, 'descend'. D-i-s...."

"No, Doreen. Larry Hempstead. 'Descend.'"

Larry Hempstead hunched to his feet from his desk, as unkempt as his handwriting, in the restless pretence of spelling the word which he did not know how to spell, surely did not wish to know how to spell, and would probably not again be called upon to spell in his entire life in Sintiempo.

"Descend," Larry mulled, added, "d . . ." and stopped. Millie left him standing for a moment, sharing his restlessness. The poster paint they had smeared on the window panes was flaking and flurrying to the baseboard, branches tied to coathooks stung the room with the smell of spruce and ponderosa pine, and there was the nervous dry slur of shoe-leather on cement. It was a mood she felt sometimes, when her voice betrayed her; when the enthusiasm strained into desperation that they did not care, and she would have shoved the grammars all together in the stove. If someone had asked her now, as someone occasionally did, "Miss Delaney, what good is this?" she would not have solemnly enumerated the good it was, but sent them off to play kickball in the sand, or to cluster into their separate sun-tanned, Indian, and Mexican hostile gigglings.

There was not by now a polished shoe in the room, nor a bookbag strap intact. Even the eternal pranks; the pigtail in the inkwell, the wart toad in the drawer, the slate caricature, the spitball surreptitiously flung; the disinterested maliciousness that classrooms individually and identically breed; even these had worn thin by now. The students in their pose circulated folded scraps of ruled manilla, grasping after subjects for the danger of illegal notes. "Doreen says Morena told her that her mother wants. . . ." "If Reed Jewett lets you borrow his horse on Saturday, why not? . . ." "For Christmas Liddie's brother says his father will. . ."

Millie in her pose brandished a blackboard pointer, the descendant no doubt of some Victorian schoolmarm's whipping stick. Her stretched smile over the spelling book was the descendant of that schoolmarm's self-important frown. The image discouraged her; the pointer jerked like a conductor's baton over a staccato allegro. The music she evoked was hardly Mozart.

"Larry, do you know what 'descend' means?"

"Yes, ma'am, it means to go down."

"Can you spell 'go down'?"

The class giggled. He could, and did. "Good enough." He sat down.

That was the afternoon that Millie first saw Miguel; after she had recited, without precedent, without plan, without any attempt to paraphrase or make it clear, the seventh book of the *Republic* of Plato. She had no illusion that the metaphor would inspire, instil, intensify; but if none of them understood a word of it, well and good. It would be her Christmas present to herself.

She went to the board and wrote "Plato". Did anyone know what it meant? No one did. Did it sound familiar? Several hands went up. She wrote "metaphor". And that? Louellen Wesch could not define it, but she could give an example. Very well. "Cave...." All of them could manage that. She pointed out Greece on the map and squandered two minutes of their waning interest on Plato's life. Then she took a long breath and a deep pause, and began, "Liken our nature in its education and want of education to a condition which I may thus describe. Picture men in an underground cave dwelling. . . ."

The unorthodoxy, the urgency, the very length of her twenty-two minute recital might have been expected to produce some unorthodox, urgent, or long reaction. But Millie, who had started with the energy of abandon, and a little melodrama, faltered as she realized that the class was rather disconcerted than impressed, and when she finished she stood kneading a blackboard eraser, in that foolishness reserved for inspiration out of place.

In the unanimous discomfort, a few faces, she saw, were making the genuine effort not to laugh. The shuffling feet had strained to a stop. The manilla messages her discipline could never quite restrain, her indiscretion had quite stilled. The only sound in the room was the scribble of Miguel Laureado's pencil on a spelling paper, and she seized on that. "Miguel, bring that paper here."

As if suddenly wakened Miguel started and stumbled out of his seat. He had never distinguished himself in any field including mischievousness, and so had never been called to the front of the room before.

From the way he clenched at the paper now, and dragged one foot behind him, Millie knew that the picture was either obscene or a caricature of her. She knew as well that she would punish him too harshly. Well, he was after all, a bad mixer; less clean and more sullen than most. His handwriting was atrocious, his accent thick and lazy; he had not been known to volunteer a single answer in his seven years at the Sintiempo School.

"Hand it to me, Miguel." He did so, his round brown face transfixed in uncalled-for terror. His hair was cut unevenly and long, straight across his forehead, and his cheekbones rose high and broad from a slender jaw, as if his whole face were conspiring to hide his eyes. But the eyes, in spite of that, confessed an abject dread. Millie looked at the paper.

Miguel's drawing of the cave was neither neat, nor artistic, nor entirely accurate, but it was unmistakably Plato's cave. It was a rough oblong that tapered up toward one end where a lopsided sun shone. In it sat a row of stick-figure prisoners, a fire behind them, a row of shadows on the opposite wall. But the logs of the fire formed a tripod, and the flame rode a double reel; the cave wall was hung with theatre drapes, and at the entrance an oblong sign proclaimed "Silver Dollar Cinema" with radiating spokes of alternating long and short pencil strokes to indicate its neon shining. Along the side he had copied from the board, "Plato Metaphor Cave" and the letters had been retraced until they ran blackly into each other. Millie looked again at the face converging at the frightened eyes, "Miguel . . ." she wonderingly began. But her softer tone rather deepened than dissolved the tension of his face, and so she handed the picture back and said, "I'll see you after class, Miguel." He stumbled back to his seat, and Millie, composed, opened the spelling book again. "Morena: 'recommend'."

He stayed in his seat when the others had gone, intently knitting his knuckles into a straight line. He gave no sign that he had noticed when Millie sat on the desk in front of him, and she, not wanting to begin wrong, watched the class retreating, running, beyond the window frame. Begrudgingly, Miguel sighed and pressed his fists against each other on the desk. " 'Descend'," he said between his teeth, "d-e-s-c-e-n-d."

"How old are you, Miguel?"

"Thirteen years old."

"You don't like school."

The boy wore a rabbit's foot and a St. Christopher medal together on a bead-chain around his thick brown neck, and slid them back and forth together, scratching the medal with the rabbit claw. "No," he said.

"Why not?"

Studying the knuckles again, he ran the tip of his tongue thoughtfully around his mouth, but said nothing. "You can tell me, Miguel. Even if it's that you don't like me."

"Oh, no!" Although this was the protest she had counted on, its explosive sincerity gratified her strangely. He sighed and said with effort, "I liked this afternoon."

"Did you understand what I was saying?"

"I think." He hesitated, then the smile broke and squeezed his eyes successfully this time almost out of sight. "Everybody spends his whole life in the Silver Dollar Cinema and never comes out, no, Miss Delaney?"

"Yes, Miguel." She remembered afternoons when, in the petty martyrdom of their apathy, she had offered her students the easy, pious voice of shallow optimism. She wanted now to apologize to Miguel for not knowing how not to be the schoolmarm they expected of her. But she could not do that.

"Can you spell all the words in the lesson?" He shrugged and nodded. "But you don't. Why not? You never look at the book in class."

"I take home the book."

"But you never look at it in class. Why do you do that?"

Miguel opened his palms and gestured feebly at the room, then shook his head and frowned, but Millie understood. "Never mind. I do it myself."

"I bring it back, Miss Delaney."

"Miguel, relax your mouth. Like this: I bring *it* back."

"I bring it back."

"Good. Miguel: do you have books at home?"

He frowned, again shrugged again. "Only the book I bring home from class."

"Would you like to have other books to take home?"

"Harder books?

"More difficult, maybe but some would have good stories."

"I would like that, yes, please. I would be careful of books—and bring them back!"

IX

The months swallowed each other toward Sintiempo's invisible summer. Geegee rocked, measuring and marking time, gritting her teeth around the harmonica frame more often than she played it, greedily disapproving Millie's protégé.

"Mexican," she would mumble, watching them on Saturday mornings where they sat over a book and cups of hot chocolate. "Never been a Mexican in this room except to clean," but the feeble protest, made against the mouth of the harmonica, came through a toneless "m-nz-nng, m-zng".

The Anglebergers, as Millie's visits became irregular and infrequent, experienced a constriction in the Saturday morning coffee hour, a tendency to vague and heightened blame.

"Millie can't make it," Lena would say, rocking the telephone receiver in her palm, stretching her lips thinly over her teeth below an aluminium helmet of rolled curlers. "Too much work to do."

"Works too hard, Millie."

"She has too much work to do," Lena repeated, placing the responsibility.

"Works too hard," said Duncan, pointedly dense.

The lawn and Duncan's round chin became somewhat more shaggy, Lena acquired a more distant and less protective tone when Millie's name was mentioned; eventually they dispensed with the coffee habit altogether. Annoyingly, the grocery boy came obediently early, earlier and earlier, arriving once before Lena was out of the curlers, which exasperated her beyond reason, all the more since she had nothing to scold him for.

"I don't see the filet, lordy I don't know what..."

"Here, Mrs. Angleberger."

"Oh. Well all right, all right then, run along."

She would lie on the fat and floral couch till noon in a chequered dressing-gown, with the *Reader's Digest* propped on her hip bone. "Duncan what have you got Millie working on?"

"Tutoring her pupils through, it seems. Says she's helping some of them at home."

"Hooo, lordy, Millie says they spend too much time in school."

"Not my idea, not my idea."

"Hoooc."

Millie worked Miguel too hard, she knew. She remembering thinking, when he had stumbled toward her in the classroom, "I will punish him too harshly," and at times she felt she had. She would not let him return a book he did not understand, but would insist, "Miguel, I know you can. Read it again." And with a small, determined squint, whether at her or the book she could not quite tell, he would take it back and read it again.

They were high moments when he understood; when, having left her with a trace of the old sullenness, he would return leaping the back porch steps, knocking with the flat of his palm as he opened the kitchen door, "Miss Delaney!" And he would recite the poem he had suddenly seen, fumble through pages looking for a paragraph he wanted to read, or greet her ecstatically in the language of the book he held in reverent and at least peremptorily scrubbed hands.

Cautiously Millie began to perceive the possibility of not being alone. Not ever having realized that sharing could have to do with more than the local topics, the spelling book, the afghans and the charity baskets, suddenly she was possessed of the power to spend an idea and see it doubled in the spending. "Too much of her is on the inside," Avril Hilton had said. Millie began to open, began to spill to Miguel's insatiable inquisitiveness beliefs she had hardly known she held, phrases she had not remembered remembering, abstract hopes she had not given even the corporeality of words. She was herself overwhelmed with the number of things he must read; images, lines, scenes, things, people wedged in her bookshelf filled her mind, and she filled Miguel's arms with too many books for a thirteen year old boy to read, which he took and read.

He returned them surreptitiously in the grocery box. He started early on Saturdays, running his whole delivery route from the Gallencamp Emporium, coming to Miss Delaney with Shakespeare under mayonnaise, intoning as he bowed and set the box down, "How now good mistress; day wears on to noon, and still hast not the pot upon the stove?" Millie applauded and set the milk on to boil. Or, sweeping the floor with the pages of *Don Juan*, self-conscious of his feat, he said, "Here, marble-willed from fools who hunt and quarry 'im, arrives our hero from the town Emporium." Laughing, almost startled, Millie sat with him to explain poetic feet, to find that he had dissected and discovered rhythm by himself. "I understand!" he said again and again, and gratefully, Millie knew he did.

Millie, who had never travelled beyond Tucson, and that only once, with her father on a solemn weekend shortly before his death; who had never seen a train but the red toy locomotive of the Railton line, imagined that this must be what travelling was like. She set off with every book, destination a receptive and responsive mind; the excitement of departure, the long lay-bys of listless waiting, the unproductive drum of the rails themselves, the hint of a city through smoky suburbs, the abrupt arrival, "I understand!" making the long trip short. She had envisioned as clearly as a picture postcard what her job, beyond Bombo and the blackboard pointer, might mean to her, and now the picture seemed at the same time flat and artificially vivid and intricately accurate. It was as a city she had read about, and knew by heart and history, which seemed on arrival wholly misrepresented by the generalizations of a foreign imagining, until, groping her way, she found in what unimagined ways the things she had been told were true after all. She explored Miguel, and came upon his ideas, adolescent but acute, as upon street signs corresponding to the labels of a map she held. And she longed more than ever urgently for the world which would be discoverable in this, more real than exciting, way.

Then she would see herself not as the traveller, but as the conductor, reassuring Miguel through a difficult journey of known terrain. The idea of conductors held her in a different way than it had as she wielded the blackboard baton, and inspired in her a new and gentle, accepting self-respect—for the official who arranges, and is not new land himself; the musician evoking but creating no sound, the wire that carries but is not electricity; for the punching of tickets, the flick of the baton, the tremble of the filament which is nothing of itself, and without which nothing is.

Miguel, for his part, saw Miss Delaney in as many lights as his task created moods. He stood at the beginning of each new subject as before an impassable mountain, and felt as he read that he gathered understanding by handfuls of pebbles; but having reached the peak, he looked back with astonishment at the ease of the distance he had come. Miss Delaney was slaver, conductor, mother, friend. He tried to express his gratitude in affection that verged sometimes on affectation, and at times he felt that he should never make her understand the size of the gift she had given him. But at others, at arbitrary moments which had little to do with his current measure of success, sometimes indeed in a very outburst of respectful love, he felt his gratitude as shallow as that of an avaricious heir. He defended Miss Delaney with passionate reverence from attacks he invented in his mind, but he used her. It was her superior knowledge that made her valuable to him, and yet he resented his own assumption of her superior mind, which silenced him at moments when he felt her wrong.

Not that they never disagreed. Miguel, thrilled by Plato's metaphor, when he came to the rest of the book found it a muddy bog of words, as he freely said, a phrase which he thought of as Dickensian. It confused without challenging him. He read for pages without following the words with anything but his eyes, until he realized abruptly that his mind was focused on something which really held no interest for him at all; the song his little sister inarticulately chanted at her solitary game outside, or the path of a moth that flurried around a bare bulb in his corner of the one-room adobe house. And when, page by page, Miss Delaney traced the argument out until she evoked a solemn and matter of fact, "I understand," he wondered still: so what?

"A quoi servir?" he pompously displayed a chapter heading he had memorized, pronouncing the French with a Mexican inflection that made it slide rising on the second and fourth syllables.

"This Glaucon—*a quoi servir*? Yes, Plato, no, Plato, just as you say, Plato. He might just go away; no difference."

"Thrasymachus challenges Plato, Miguel."

"Thrasymachus, pooh!" He spoke as if Thrasymachus were Louellen Wesch. "Thrasymachus is a fat fool. You could have answered Thrasymachus, Miss Delaney." He negated the insincerity of his compliment by adding explosively, "I could answer Thrasymachus: look here, fat fool! No. I am supposed to think that Glaucon is a bright good boy: bright, white, blanco, blank. Would anybody answer in such a way?"

"It's a convention of the dialectic, Miguel."

"A bad convention. It is not real."

"No convention is 'real'. That's what convention means."

Miguel smiled, the private smile that shoved his flushed cheeks up to the fringe of black lash, thinking of his mother's midnight convention before the grimy altar of a chipped plaster madonna, the unreal way she taught his silent, sullen sister to kneel with her black hair fanning her shoulders and brushing her clasped and stubby little fists. "That is true," he said in the submissive tone of Glaucon.

"And Plato is searching for a different kind of reality."

"Ah! A table in the sky!"

"No, Miguel, you don't understand."

"I do!" he flashed with incredible mobility of the round, flat face. He did not mind, indeed, enjoyed with the neat satisfaction of logic, when Miss Delaney proved him wrong. But he could not bear to be thought of as making idle protestations, misunderstanding objections like fat Thrasymachus.

"This table is a picture at the Silver Dollar Cinema," he retreated to his old successful metaphor. "And only God knows how to work the movie camera. Ha! Do you know the O'Odham think that when it storms God has a head cold, and he is sneezing when it thunders? Is that not equally foolish? Yes! Let me play Glaucon. I say," he thundered his fist with adolescent majesty on the oaken table, causing Geegee to moan an "m-nz-ng" through the bass end of her harmonica, "I say this table is real, and when it thunders it is because the lightning burns up the air and makes a ferocious wind (this was a fact from the science primer of several years before) and this book is real, and Plato was real, but what he says is nothing but sneezing!"

And so she set him on to Berkeley and Boswell, to the account of Sam Johnson kicking the rocks to prove the existence of matter. And at this Miguel imprisoned his eyes with the depth of his delighted laugh, and went for weeks chuckling and stubbing his toes on the stones in the path of his grocery route.

Class at first was a different matter; or, rather, class was the same. He kept the pretence of indifference, shuttling scrawled mistakes forward among the collected papers, staring at his knuckles, professing ignorance. He did not distinguish himself in anything including mischievousness; he was a bad mixer, less clean and more sullen than most. On examinations he left more blanks than he filled, his handwriting was atrocious, his accent. . . .

His accent imperceptibly dissolved. From among the slurrings and slipshod vowels, the dropped g's and nasal interferences, from the scrambled grammar of the sun-tanned, Mexican and Indian indifferences of the class, to which before, Miguel had added a low, infrequent and congruous note; his voice began to emerge, no more frequent, no less low, but clear and careful, showing the filtered mark of Mrs. Milton Delaney's Illinois precision.

Millie had meticulously neglected any mention of his conduct in the classroom. Whatever pains she might have taken to make him imitate the forming of an Anglo-Saxon S or T, however rigorously she may have forced him to the understanding of an idea three thousand years behind and ten years ahead of him, she had not questioned his conspiracy to learn without its being known. Her discretion Miguel rewarded when, finding that no formidable recognition descended upon him as his pronunciation improved, he began to feign not apathy but an aggressive naïveté, and then to make consciously absurd and even obscure contributions. One morning without preface or apparent plan he raised his hand, rose and reeled ecstatically through the entire "Perceval, or, the Story of the Grail", which was contained in a book of medieval romances Millie had given him the previous Saturday. He told it in simple but interminable detail, epilogued it, "That's an old Spanish tale my mother tells", though he had dwelt with particular care on the Welsh intricacies of dress, and sat down. This could not very well be ignored, but as Miss Delaney only smiled blandly and thanked him, the class could not be entirely sure that they had not missed a request of some kind for Miguel to tell the story. That, or perhaps he had successfully deluded Miss Delaney in his consuming of this half hour that might otherwise have been tediously spent over the multiplication table. In which case, he ought to be something of a hero; but they could not go so far as to treat him as one, because it might after all be that he was only a little more stupid than they had thought, and that Miss Delaney was sorry for him. So they did nothing. That day Miguel turned in a blank geography quiz which, promising herself that she would not again so far let herself be charmed from discipline, she graded 100 per cent and returned. She sketched on his paper the stick figure of a Mexican boy with high apple cheeks and a shock of black hair obscuring his grin, holding aloft a rough outline of Perceval's grail, and he accepted the paper with a convulsive explosion of muffled glee, not daring to raise his head.

When she called on him to spell "cerebral", he spelled "Boethius", over whom they had spent two Saturday hours and half a box of cocoa not half a dozen days before. Beginning with Louellen Wesch, they emitted an indecisively derisive and small snicker, and Millie, helpless before the illogic of her pride, laughed more loudly than any of them and called on Louellen Wesch.

Miguel was at this time happier than he had been or had dreamed of being, and with an inevitability he did not comprehend as such, his anxieties increased to equal his happiness in kind and measure. Alone, he had believed his mind of an unmatched activity and acuteness, and now that Miss Delaney seemed to confirm his belief, its occasional periods of obstinate lassitude seemed as well unprecedented, even unique. When he rehearsed to himself the facts of his existence; his age, his partial support of two ignorant women, his fulltime attendance at school, his late nights and early mornings in the squalor of the adobe room, rounding his young shoulders over the pages of adult books, he was overwhelmed with his own virtue. But at the same time he recognized these reflections as of the same stamp as his mother's pious endurance, and he was angry with her for his inheritance of the tendency to them. It seemed not simply lazy but sinful that, when he was not even tired, his mind could range from the difficult page, that this could happen even over the light, the "unimportant" books of Dickens, in whom he delighted. He tried, an indiscretion on Millie's part, to read Henry James, and thought it such tedious folly that he was sure his mind was deficient of some vital subtlety. If, after a struggle over passages he only half-grasped in a way that made him feel only half-awake, or only half-alive, he suddenly had a bright and original idea, he scribbled this idea in the margin to repeat to Millie Delaney, and felt that by delighting her he deceived her as to the heavy fog that went before and after his inspiration. In spite of which, if, as occasionally happened, she scolded him for the inaccuracy of his observation, he felt himself violently misunderstood, and his thoughts pouted behind a masque of obedient embarrassment. But it never occurred to him that Miss Delaney, too, might have felt and still feel an indolence beyond her will in the very study she most loved.

For his fourteenth birthday in early February, Miss Delaney gave him a notebook of his own, a plain rich black leather folder and a hundred sheets of more elegant paper than he had ever seen, heavy unruled bond as smooth and white as polished marble, and smelling of the clean freshness of new-baked bread. He inscribed his name in careful letters on the first page and pasted, as introduction, the spelling paper with Plato's cave in the upper corner of the next. Gratified by his excessive pleasure, she gave him the next week a sleek black pen, and the beautiful very emptiness of his book lured its point, lured him to transcribe his criticism of the things he read, and to implant in a tidying hand the sights he observed on his grocery walk, to practise the idioms of ancient poets.

"Mrs. Hilton is peanut butter spread on moldy bread," he wrote beneath the date 2.24.43. He crossed out "moldy" and wrote "raisin" above it. He crossed out "butter" and substituted "crunch". "Mrs. Hilton is peanut crunch spread on raisin bread." He exchanged "is" for "was", which suggested more of a narrative and less of a personal prank. He tried to remember her first name: Annie, Ada, Ava, was that right? "Ava Hilton was peanut crunch spread on raisin bread." He crossed out the whole thing and with an impulsive gesture crossed out the date as well. He drew a dotted line with the broad nib of his pen. Avril, that was it.

"2.24.43."

"Avril Hilton's face was made in the mould of a cooky tin. Her raisin eyes shone through a layer of peanut butter heavily spread."

Although his notebook was the most private possession Miguel had ever had, so that with unnecessary precaution he tucked it under the mattress of his tin cot when he left home, he was greedy enough for Miss Delaney's approval to insure her free access to its pages. She approved its many cross-hatchings and the care and frequency of his re-attempts, which Miguel assured her were as difficult as they looked. He hoped, he said, that in time it would become easier. Miss Delaney smiled a gentle smile that balanced her discouraging words, doubting that this was true.

"I don't suppose it gets easier, Miguel. It gets better."

And this was a sort of challenge that made Miguel's brain soar. He was in the first flush of a love affair with words, and when told that he could use them well, he baulked and doubted and felt himself feigning, but when assured of the difficulty of his desire, there was no height he could not attain, nor anything that he would not forego to attain it.

He had one week a book of Pope and some passages of Shelley assigned, and he remarked to Miss Delaney that the former would have thought the latter a fraud. Miss Delaney said, "Oh, yes, of course," and dismissed it as self-evident. But Miguel had meant more than that. He was fascinated with his ability to guess that a man would detest something that did not exist in his own lifetime, and even questioned whether it was true, since it could not be proven, unless in a heaven which might very well not exist either.

"3.4.43."

> *"Oh that these lawless frauds were what they seem:*
> *Oh, that the dream-inducers were the dream!*

He was particularly pleased with this imitation, and assured Miss Delaney, although he was not much moved by Shelley, that he was no fonder of Pope's rules, and that the sentiments of the verse were no more his than the style.

His own eagerness and Millie's, though she thought more of Augustan ideals than he did, destroyed all moderation in teacher and taught. He read too much and too fast, assimilating as he appreciated, only in brief, bright passages and striking lines. His incredible hunger began to be sated toward spring. Although physically well, he became ill of a restlessness, under the strain of changed and forced routine. In May he read less and wrote more, wrote as he read and remembered, in bright, brash fragments. In spite of Millie's warning, it became easier, but not steadily easier. Sometimes he went for days, more intensely agitated than ever before December in the hours spent in the classroom, without drawing his notebook from under the mattress, and then he would sit all one night on the bed, his brown back propped against the warm adobe, the notebook propped on his warm bare knees, playing games with a single word, or wrenching a sentence to almost fit some caustic vision he had had of a Sintiempo scene.

Millie never failed in amazement at his precocity. She thought there was the potential of true talent in him, and thought so with much greater consistency than his own fitful conceit of genius. But she too became suspicious of the brevity of his inspiration. She implored him to stick to some idea, to write her a story, or a whole poem. She pointed out that his endless metaphors seemed to lessen the things they described; that he saw trivial things in nature, rather than nature in the trivial, or in nature, the divine: the palm tree was a spouting fountain pen, eyes could be fragments of broken glass. She thought it wrong. There was nothing, perhaps, of Plato in it, and too little of her idea of a child. And his idiom rasped against her sense of beauty.

We are curiously insensitive about the effects of our tangible possessions upon our heirs. Our characters, our good works leave an impression more profound, perhaps, but those at least we pay the homage of imagination, seeing our goodness and our philosophies filtering into posterity with a kind of slowly fading grace. Even money, which is after all the least material of objects, to be made use of with greater freedom and variety than any remnant of experience or thought, inspires us with a reassuring sense of the surviving. But objects seem weightless weights, which can have no value to their inheritors beyond a shopworn usefulness. If an obscure professor of Latin in an Illinois University in 1901 had known that his rather archaic taste in poetry would create a profound distress in the heart of an obscure Mexican boy forty years and a thousand miles away, he might well have added the works of Baudelaire and Verlaine, at least a *Don Quixote* to his library, in which case Millie might have thought to discuss the phenomenon of translation. As it was, all the books she offered him were in English, and Miguel assumed them to be written in English. Also, Milton Delaney was an old man in 1901. His tastes ran to Wordsworth, rather more to Rossetti, and rather to Elizabeth Barrett than Robert Browning.

Millie therefore set before Miguel the example of the late Victorians as the most modern poetry her library contained. Miguel came of his own accord, with the perpetual astonishment of lonely youth, to the ragged idiom of the twentieth century, but he was convinced like Millie Delaney that it could not be valid.

"Write a whole poem, Miguel. Never mind if it's imperfect. But it will be a start of another kind, don't you see?"

"I can't," he said in both distress and rebellion.

"I know you can." She showed him Rossetti and Tennyson. "I don't mean to imitate; use your own words. But make it simple, and make it rhyme. Copy the forms. Only describe something, if you like, but make it a whole description that begins and ends, and doesn't set out to destroy all the beauty that's there. Write something gentle, and complete."

"I can't."

"You need to, Miguel. I know, I know you can write a beautiful poem."

He did not know it. But he knew that it must be good advice. And he wanted desperately not to lose her good opinion. Even when he thought her wrong, or prim, or too exacting, it was his one sure goad, his one defence against an unproductive loneliness. He tried and failed, and turned out tedious, difficult pages of primroses wilting into calico, people grotesquely turned of tin. He brooded and bit his fingernails, stubbed without laughing at the stones in his path, destroyed all the ant beds from Mesquite to Ocotillo with a bitter twist of his huaracha, and he could be seen on Saturdays, early, shouldering a carton of raw food, with a tight furrow above his eyes, distractedly humming snatches of his mother's Spanish lullaby.

What this concern, absurdity, and subterfuge, these not really secret Saturday mornings and not very remarkable classroom pranks and not earth-shaking notebook pages brought Millie Delaney cannot be certain. But if the remarkable transformation and vacillation of the mind of the son of a Sintiempo cleaning woman went unnoticed, the town was not so dull as to miss the subtle change in Millie Delaney. Avril Hilton of the raisin eyes cannot be said to have lived up to the perception of her earlier remark, and only succeeded in observing that Millie Delaney "seemed happier" lately. It was Mrs. Angleberger who, in response to this imprecision, predicted, "My word, Avril, more than that. Jumpy more like. Hoooo, more than high time Millie Delaney had a beau."

And in more than high time, the calendar having turned a new leaf on to June, June brought Miguel's poem, Geegee's death, and Karl Ormerod from the quarry.

Karl Ormerod left Railton when, in May, the eldest son of Vernon Smee turned eighteen, and was sent for by the recruiting office in Tucson. He was no more involved in the family chagrin than a boarder who keeps pretty much to himself is apt to be, but he felt uncomfortable among the draftboard talk at the dinner table, as if sooner or later he was bound to invite some attention, by either his silence or his remarks. He was bored with his work anyway, which had all the monotony of the Houston bank without any of its comfort. Then, too, there was a dark chiquita who had lovely eyes, but the length of whose nose was beginning to irk him. Dark girls had always been drawn to Karl with a singularly possessive force, as the sea leaps after a bright sky. This one was beginning to make claims on him, and her brother rather glowered from the lettuce shed.

So he left with as little disturbance as possible, which means without collecting the ten days' pay due him, and begged a ride in the railroad yard from one of the quarry truckers.

Work in the quarry was plentiful enough, for the reasons that Vernon Smee had enumerated, and the foreman on Lenajidak took Karl on, not without some hesitation concerning the air of the indoors that he perceived in the pale young man. The workers sensed it too, and because they liked him well enough, tended to be condescendingly kind to him, asking now and again in broken phrases of his own tongue how much of a load he wanted to carry, how many of the dynamite fuses he could handle by himself. To such questions Karl answered, "Todo!" with some annoyance, and was therefore nicknamed "Todo" by his good-natured compañeros, who when they pronounced his whole name, elided it into: "Todormerod". So he became known as "Toad", which he did not mind because it fitted him so poorly, and because he seldom minded anything.

On a Saturday in early June, on the road from the quarry to the town, he had passed the solitary mustard house in the yucca dell, and leaned against a tall palm, rolling his back against its rough bark with a pleasant sensation of warmth and strength, smoking a cigarette with his right fingers from the left side of his mouth.

The back door of the big house opened, and a Mexican boy with four thick books tucked under one arm and an empty cardboard carton swinging at the end of the other, backed down the steps with his head tilted to one side, talking to a slender girl who leaned against the doorjamb and brushed her fine black hair back from her forehead to one side. As he watched, the hand on her hair dipped freely away in a salute, and the boy turned and took a few steps away from her, around the corner of the house and in the direction of the mountain. Suddenly he dropped both box and books in the dust, retraced his steps at a run and flung his arms around the woman, with such force that they both stumbled slightly back into the house before she braced herself against the impact. Their laughter, his a young, low giggle and hers a higher music of abandon, travelled the still air as the sight of the mountains, undulating one behind the other, strikingly clear, deceptively far. The boy sprang away as quickly as he had landed, scooped the books into the box and stumbled on with them along the uphill road to the Mexican village. "Good-bye, good-bye, Miss Delaney!" he called over his shoulder, and her clear voice sounded, "Till Monday," after him.

She leaned still against the door, still fingering the fine hair with a graceful motion, smiling with closed eyes into the sun. She swayed away then, so slightly that one could not have said that she had been still before, or was now in motion, stepped into the patio and raised one hand gently to a yucca blossom and slowly and faster twirled, until her hair and her skirt and her outspread arms made cartwheels about the slender stalk of her body. She sank all at once into a soft stretch of grass, lay on the full-flung circle of her skirt, clasped her hands behind her head, and seemed to sleep.

Karl was deeply stirred by the scene, though if he had been accompanied he might have remarked, "Not bad", and considered the phrase adequate expression of his feelings. He started toward the girl for almost the distance between two palms, then with a subtlety and deviousness unusual for him where women were concerned, he retreated quietly toward town, only repeating to himself the name Miss Delaney.

He had little enough trouble finding out her first name, her job, her connection with the founder of the quarry, and the curious mixture of indulgence and awe with which she was regarded. Sintiempo's unmixed enthusiasm discouraged him a bit, made him suspicious and finally almost certain that he would find the girl distastefully prim. But looking over the situation in Sintiempo, as he phrased it to himself, it seemed that Millie Delaney was worth a try. And so he watched her from a distance over the mountain and over the Sintiempo crowds until the old woman, her guardian and step-great-grandmother, was buried on June 20th.

XI

At Millie's only gentle hinting, Miguel chose the bunting and oleander background of commencement for his self-unveiling. He told her with unaccountable formality on a Saturday morning near the end of school, that he would, at the graduation, have something to say. With efficient solemnity Millie agreed to make the arrangements, and notwithstanding some misgiving on the part of Superintendent Angleberger (seventh graders did not usually speak at commencement, and young Laureado did not usually speak at all), this was done.

Millie's class contained fourteen eighth-graders and twelve seventh-graders. She passed all of the latter on to the eighth, and all of the former she graduated; some of them because they sometimes tried, some of them because they could have passed if they had sometimes tried, some of them because their parents needed them at home, some of them because another year at the Sintiempo school would have made no difference anyway. Louellen Wesch she appointed, of course, valedictorian.

114

Graduation was held in a parched cemented corner of the playing field; the backstop basket-woven with strands of lavender and yellow crepe, a platform faced with rows of the temporarily potted fronds of frontyard palms, the bleachers greenly new-enamelled to merit the formal organdy and corded bottoms of the graduates.

They gathered before the ceremony in the auditorium at noon on June 16th, a record June 16th for heat, *The Sintiempo Sun* disclosed. Humidity was thirty-four, the *Sun* reported, high for Sintiempo, and high for June. Heat and humidity seemed to slide from the ring of mountain slopes to the grounds and the thinly windowed room, and to concentrate itself at the congregated armpits. Flocked rayon taffeta was in that year. By an oversight of the local ready-to-wear apparel, Maria Elena de la Iglesia wore the same stiff flowered frock in white that Louellen wore in blue. Louellen cried, and going for a handkerchief, dropped her valedictory address in the cloakroom ventilator grate. Superintendent Angleberger, on his knees, retrieved it a page at a time with a piece of chewing-gum lowered on a string. The pages stuck together after that, and obliterated several vital words which Louellen could not remember. The seventh graders, who were to distribute programmes and carry the diplomas forward for presentation, came in from the former task with mimeograph ink on their hands and started a game of touch-tag on the auditorium stage. Larry Hempstead, in pursuit of Dadie Fouzel, left an ink-print in the small of her back on a satin sash. Dadie cried, and shoved Larry into the diploma stand, which emptied its carefully sorted contents across the auditorium floor. Mr. Angleberger, with a piece of chewing-gum on his heel, trod on a ribbon-wrapped certificate, cursed "Godzooks" in front of his students, and was restrained from whipping Larry by the firm hand of Lena on his elbow and the soothing voice of Millie in his ear. The ruined diploma was Morena Garcia's. Morena cried. Lena, cooing, implanted a congratulatory kiss on the left side of each of the fourteen faces, and fourteen kisses coagulated on the honoured cheeks.

"Jesus Gawd," said Avril Hilton, diluting orangeade for the reception after the spectacle, "why can't they do this sort of thing at night?"

Miguel arrived late, flushed and silent, his corduroy pockets bulging with the tensing of his fists. Millie greeted him casually, but clasped her hands before her, waist high, in secretive encouragement, at which he dropped his eyes.

"Is your mother coming?"

"She can't." He had not asked her.

He walked at the end of the procession, behind Louellen Wesch and in front of Harold Tso, who carried a guitar strung from his shoulders on a beaded strap. Duncan followed at the end, rather out of sorts, twitching an official smile of pride and poking at his glass-rims with a little finger. A phonograph on the outside platform, an old wind-up type, since the electric cord wouldn't reach, was manned by a flustered mother in a damp blue crêpe. Its heavy Pomp and Circumstance ran down and died with a groan just as the graduates reached the track hurdles that lined their processional aisle. An erratic music of flies and mosquitoes drew out the dying drone until the flustered mother's husband leaped to an energetic pumping of the Victoria crank, and was applauded with much familiar humour and cries of, "Attaboy, Nick," and "Save the day".

The day was warping under a heavy sun; minor mirages rose from the metal chairs, and programmes fanned in ink-smudged fingers;

younger siblings set up a whine and were stuffed with sticky peppermints from their mothers' bags. The graduates stumbled into the bleachers; Louellen, Miguel, Harold and Duncan mounted the platform; Pomp and Circumstance broke off abruptly with the zipping sound of a needle scratch, and Harold Tso played the national anthem on his guitar.

As the congregation stood and sang—Doreen Sammon, who considered that she played the guitar as well as Harold Tso, loud and consciously off key—Millie surveyed from her side front seat the circle of graduates, speakers and spectators. Nearly all Sintiempo was there, collectively proud and collectively overwarm. Her love for Miguel diffused itself in the radiating heat, and spread to the edges of the hymning crowd. A child behind her, surfeited of peppermints, had begun to toy with the coins in his mother's purse, and was dropping them one by one, aiming at her toes, from which they slid and clunked in the dust. "I'll knock some sense into you," the mother hissed at last, after a few remonstrances whispered beneath the song. And her remark filled Millie with deep satisfaction, as a definition of the event. Sintiempo had gathered to pay its own brand of homage to knowledge, and it was a matter of some significance that those who bore life by bludgeoning were willing to put the bludgeon at learning's disposal. She, too, was proud, and overwarm.

Three small boys with yellow teeth paraded banner-bearing in and set the flags of the nation, the state and the school in standards rooted on the platform. The graduates led the audience in a recitation of the pledge of allegiance, and Harold Tso played "Semper fidelis" on the guitar.

"Ladies and gentlemen, parents, brothers and sisters, friends, graduates and honoured guests," Duncan addressed the assembly from a bunting-draped podium, "we gather today. . . ." He spoke for a remarkable length of time, and these words were in his speech: honour, progress, proud, prosperity, posterity, threshold, unsurpassed. Patriotic, troubled times, history, future, beauty, brotherhood, pursuit, hope, career, commencement. Momentous, auspicious, religious, ambitious, whatever, however, wherever, and quarry. He cited the words of God, Herodotus, Thomas Jefferson, Milton Delaney. His address was enthusiastically approved.

Louellen, freckled and damp, chubby and ringleted, spoke of the shrinking size of the schoolground playing field as she had grown in her eight years crossing it to the morning bell. She reminisced twelve minutes' worth of schoolroom juvenilia with counterfeit nostalgia, and when she came to the obliterated words in her text, ingeniously substituted an appeal for a round of applause for Millie Delaney. The audience complied, her words were enthusiastically approved, and Harold Tso played the "Mommy and Daddy Waltz" on the guitar.

Miguel came stiffly to the podium from his tin-backed chair. Watching his finger-tips grasp slowly at the unaccustomed stiffness of his cuffs, Millie begged, Oh, God, let them think him wonderful, and her fingers rubbed at her peacock cotton skirt in imitation of his own. Behind the podium he squintingly and uncertainly smiled to Millie, to a perspiring audience beginning to squirm in anticipation of diluted orangeade.

"The Dove," he said awkwardly, "by Miguel Laureado." His voice was staccato cool and high in his special care, lifting from the aftermath of stale guitar.

"White dove, snow dove
Drifted to the river brink,
Fallen to the river brink,
Drifted to the bank to drink,
Snow dove, come with me.

"I have come far, come far,
Come far on a wounded winging,
Travelled the lily-coloured wing
On a wind worn sad of singing.

"White dove, snow dove
Melting at the river bank,
Moaning at the river brink,
Bring your wounded wing and song,
Snow dove, come with me.

"I am alone, alone,
Alone and without master,
Without a love alone
And in a foreign town.

"Snow dove, come to me,
Weeping at the river brink.
Lily, river, love and I
Weeping at the river brink
For your wounded wing and singing.
We will find you wings to fly."

Much later, looking back, remembering with what sweet absurdity Miguel's white dove had fallen into the lavender crêpe and palm fronds, Millie saw the afternoon as the elusive pivot point of all her days. For all its being out of tone, and surely it was that, Miguel's poem had not jarred as her own classroom recitation of Plato had. Neither, of course, were the good parents of Sintiempo absolutely overwhelmed, but their applause outlasted the clapping awarded the guitar. Perspiring faces under poppy-covered hats sought each other nodding, with eyelids lifted and lips compressed, as if to say, "Who would have thought it?" At the back of the assembly, one of the workmen from the quarry (a new one, from the paleness of his skin; God knows why he was there) said "Bravo!" twice, and Miguel regained his seat in lash-lowered confusion, furtively searching for Millie's face. Distracted through the diploma-handing, the recessional, the reception, she avoided publicly acknowledging him, but composed the words that must wait for Saturday, to convince him of his promise, and her pride.

But then, unfittingly, ill-timed, so unexpectedly that it lent (she did not say this, not
even wholly to herself) an aura of the trivial,
that afternoon Geegee died.

Millie came home to find her sitting,
breathing with difficulty in the heavy dark,
staring unseeing straight ahead with a small,
sour expression. She flung open the windows
and doors and helplessly offered a tumbler of
water from the warm tap, but the water was
ignored and the doors invited only a stirring of
more damp heat. Geegee made no sound but a
faintly rasping moaning, like the feeble "m-nz-
nng" of an old harmonica.

Millie called the clinic, and Geegee was
removed from her grandson's house for the first
time in seventeen years, on a sheetless
stretcher, her ankles hanging over its end, her
heavily booted useless feet bobbing the pattern
of the rutted road. In the painful white of the
clinic room, low medical tones discussed a
removal to a modern hospital, but Railton's
clinic was not much better than Sintiempo's,
Tucson was a hundred miles by road. It did not
take a professional eye to see that Geegee
wouldn't last the trip.

She did not last until the sun of a record heat for June 16th had died behind the quarry peak, and Millie watched, rather than heard, the whistling breath from that sunken mouth subside. She tried to make herself aware that she was watching death, but Miguel's dove, too much alive, was too much on her mind. The bubbles that rose to the wrinkled rim of Geegee's mouth came ever smaller and thicker, the lash-long down of her upper lip fluttered more faintly, and one tear of saliva retreated to her pillow. The hands of the meters fell, acknowledging her death; Geegee's own hands' pulse-beat acknowledged it, and a nurse solemnly, decorously drew her index and middle fingers over the flat pewter eyes. The lids clenched shut, withered into the sockets as if over toothless gums. And the easy, expected tearblur through which Millie saw that familiar, unfamiliar face distorted it, abstracted it until she could not recognize which clenched chasm was the eye, which slit might open on two rows of even artificial teeth. What right, Millie wondered with an indignation strangely static and detached, what right had this impersonal nurse in her efficient pompousness, to send an old woman darkly to the grave, to lie eternally in a pretence of hungry sleep. I shall have to let them know, she resolved, I shall have to remember when the time comes, to let them know to bury me with my eyes open.

The altar was faced with rows of the temporarily potted stalks of florist's lilies, the choir in rayon taffeta sat to the left on the benches of a mahogany loft, and Mrs. Charles D. Tso played "Nearer, My God, to Thee" on the organ. Nearly all Sintiempo was there, collectively mournful, collectively overwarm. The Reverend Neville Lemming spoke from a lavender velvet-draped podium, and these words were in his sermon: honour, posterity, threshold, unsurpassed. Future, beauty, brotherhood, hope, commencement. Religious, whatever, however, wherever, and heaven. He cited the words of God, Paul, Billy Sunday and Milton Delaney. His words were reverently approved.

And from the bunting and palm fronds of commencement; through the crepe and lilies of the funeral, Millie felt no further from the old woman in death than in life, nor in a different way: the body stiffly here and real, the soul elusive, shadowy, somewhere not to be known.

In fact, so simply and so quickly did those three days pass, that Millie was not in the least surprised, leaving the funeral rite, to see the same young quarry worker who had stood at the edge of the graduation audience, standing at the edge of this one. He was watching her, holding at a slight angle a pale face both delicately formed and ludicrously small for the height and power of his body. Millie smiled, as sadly as she felt she must, meaning to thank him for his "Bravo!"

As it was not until the moment when, as sadly as he felt he must, he returned her smile, that Millie realized the emptiness of the rooms at home, the sudden gifts that Geegee's death had given her; aloneness, and the unknown lot of liberty.

Things

XII

"**A**nd then," said Lena, "the boy came back to the Emporium for a pound and a half of bitter-sweet cooking chocolate. A pound and a half! And took it right back to her, all that way. Lordy. What do you think of that?"

"What is it, illegal or what?"

"But don't you see? What would a woman do with making brownies four days after a funeral, all alone and all. Is it a time for pastry?"

"Maybe it was toll house cookies." Duncan was perched puffing on the corner of a kitchen chair, smearing greasy flakes of bootblack on his funeral and commencement shoes. "Use bittersweet for toll house cookies, don't you?"

"Land, Duncan, are you listening? A pound and a half? And even if it was, still and all, even then, is it a time for pastry?"

"S'matter with toll house cookies?"

"Avril Hilton sent her a batch of peanut butter, for lord's sake, and she had a pie on

Thursday from Mrs. Wesch. And after ordering two barbecuing steaks and a nine pound ham? Have you ever known Millie Delaney to eat a whole barbecue steak in her entire life?”

“No,” Duncan took up a drying shoe and a stiff-bristled brush and swiped the two together obliquely like a pair of cymbals. He thought a little taste for gossip a good healthy sign in a woman, but he did not like meddling where Millie Delaney was concerned, even when the speculation took on an indulgent and friendly tone. There was something of the commercial in it, like bottling June Bugs. “Nope,” he admitted however, “never have.”

“And then to send the boy after it, a mile yonder and back. Wouldn’t you say that was queer?”

“Maybe she’s making brownies for the boy.”

“Or toll house cookies,” Lena sneered. “Not likely. Is that like Millie Delaney?”

“Don’t know why not. Heart a gold.”

“Yes, yes, but not that way. Not making cakes for people. Watch your trousers; lordy, now you’ve done it.”

Duncan had streaked black brushstrokes on his gabardine knees. “Drat,” he sighed, “dratidrat.” Lena very nearly covered her teeth with the lengthening of her upper lip. She fetched a bottle marked "Carbona" and ripped the seat out of a pair of ragged flannel drawers, then kneeled with angular effort on the linoleum and scrubbed at her husband with the spot remover, viciously, as if she could melt out his protests. Duncan submitted, waving the brush and the shoe aloft, twitching his nose against the mixed pungency of bootblack and benzine.

"She was proud of the boy. Quite right too."

"Quite right too, but a nine pound ham? And besides, the boy seemed put out somewhat having to go back all that way. Would a boy like that mind walking a mile for a batch of cookies?"

"Or a pan of fudge," Duncan enlarged the possibilities lamely.

"Avril didn't talk to Gallencamp himself. Unbend your knee. Stay still! But Mrs. Gallencamp was telling about it to Kep Hilton's secretary, and she said there was enough food in that order to keep a sieged city."

"Hearsay," Duncan mumbled. "Don't know Gallencamp should be complaining about that."

"Complaining! Hooo. Who's complaining, sir? No one's com*plain*ing. We're Delighted!" She lifted toward Duncan a toothful of delight in curious harmony with the bootblack smell. "Millie Delaney's got a beau."

XIII

As if spring were a climate of the human heart, which bursts with the year only where the year of the world is well-ordered; as if in a land where unguided spring must spend its frail haphazard colour in an angry sun, the heart unguided too must try its bloom; as if it had, even in Sintiempo June, been spring, Millie flowered with the passing of all of the withered and the wintering in her life.

The old woman had died, perhaps, as an aged tree would die, gnarled, magnificent in nothing but its silence, obediently mourned by anyone not wholly imperceptive to the value of having lasted; but leaving by its death a wider reach of sky, a deeper richness of the soil, to nourish the tender tangle at its feet. So wholly had Geegee lived in the nature of an object, so indivisibly appeared as of the furniture of the house, as familiar, as little taken into account as the fine, complaining rocking chair where she sat, that Millie had not at all realized how, in her life, the old woman counted. She had not known, because there had been before no interruption of it, how by the mere fact of existence her guardian had powerfully and subtly fulfilled the duty of that formal office. It now appeared that the technicalities had been all on the other side; that Millie had owned the house outright by the terms of her father's will, but had held it in fief from its ancient inhabitant, who preserved without doing anything to preserve, the frailty of her mother and the authority of her father. She had known in the terms of accounts and deeds, of exact figures and unquestionable documents, the extent of her possessions, but now for the first time she felt herself an owner, almost a miser, in total possession of things, of a place, of a position, above all, of her will.

She stood, on the afternoon of Geegee's funeral, in a black lawn dress that failed of severity and sorrow by the billowing lightness of its folds and the frivolous grace of its full sleeves, drawing her short gloves from her hands and smoothing them, thoughtfully, finger by finger, on the arched back of the sofa. Arranged so, the gloves seemed poised in a grasp, in an inanimate gesture of possession. She laid her hands beside them, feeling the texture of the worn needlepoint as if the sense of touch itself were the privilege of ownership. Leaving a faint heelstain of cemetery grass along the carpet, she moved to the delicate round table that her father had brought, carefully preserved in straw, from the refinement of another world. With more perhaps of her father's tendency than she would have confessed, to credit the inanimate with human power, she fingered the fragile fluting and marble tuberoses at its circumference with such a hand as she might have touched her mother's cheek. It was the thing most concretely remaining of her mother, as the quarry most insistently attested to her father's having been. And yet it was not of death that she was thinking, not even when she took Geegee's battered harmonica from the table-top and unsentimentally deposited it in the sideboard drawer. Not of death, but of objects, not even of living memory, but of the tangible remembrances which belie the obsession of a given life. Of the souvenirs of the soul. Of the quarry, her father, and the table, her mother, both of the same cool, solid substance; the one vast, unpolished, difficult to move, the other artful, proper, crafted into brittleness. She knew that she had not loved the house, and that she loved it now. And she knew that this was because now, like her life, whatever in it had been passed to her through other hands, was wholly hers, to do with as her whim predicted and her happiness required. She staggered a bit perhaps with the weight of it, floundered at the immensity of her little power. But she felt too a new respect for herself, a responsibility if you like, but no longer the passive responsibility of doing nothing to injure the memory and respect of her elders; a positive responsibility to do something to warrant a respectful memory of herself. To make a beginning, she would rearrange the furniture.

That night there were letters yet to be written, letters to mid-western relatives she had never seen or heard from, and would never write again, whose addresses she now might if she liked rip from the little leather pad and destroy. Not being mournful, nor they in need of condolence, she wrote them in the mournful terms of stock condolences, using the phrase "passed away", which she disliked, but which seemed in reference to her step-great-grandmother's inert life and casual disappearance, more accurate than the word "died". On these and on the commercial trivialities of the funeral she spent her evening, very much and very satisfactorily alone, carefully restraining herself from a regret of callousness, for fear of the greater fault of insincerity. But before she went to bed she laid a mental plan for the rearrangement of the house: the living room was too full, the drapes were too heavy for the weather or her mood, the books from the side wall and the stairwell should be relocated on the left of the mantel, so that they should command the whole of the largest wall of the room. Indeed, of her vague plans only this was certain, that the books, which had always been hers alone, should be ranged in the most imposing space of all that was now hers. She dressed in her own small room for bed, in the quaint blue satin nightgown that fell from her young breast as water rippling along a slender brook, and then, as mistress of the house, she went to the master bedroom which had been empty since her mother's death, and slept soundly, with the wide free soundness of luxurious space, in the deep bed of that upstairs room.

She slept soundly, and yet she dreamed, a dream that was rather felt and heard than seen, of vast cool space, of waves of lily-coloured air through which she floated in an effortless flight, beckoned by a sound of gentle wind through the fronds of blowing palms. She rose buoyantly to a heaven that withdrew for her, ever lighter and warmer, and she woke with her face in a square of sun that the open window framed on her pillow. The air was divested of the damp of the last few days; a mockingbird in low flight among the pyracantha bushes called up a shrill chatter of wakefulness; a yucca reaching just above the window-sill beckoned gently with its handful of tremulous amber blossoms. It was Sunday. She rose leaping, flinging the sheet away from her so that it billowed and spread and settled with animal langour on the sunlit floor. She dressed excitedly in a pair of slim white slacks and a loose shirt, bolted a cup of coffee and two peanut butter cookies, and then in a breathless hurry she did not quite try to understand, began haphazardly dragging books from the shelves of the stairwell and stacking them in the middle of the floor.

When Miguel arrived she was sitting in the midst of them cross-legged, resting from her onslaught of the side wall shelves with a volume of *Childe Harold* in her hands. Harold's travels, however, were only the catalyst of her own. She was remembering again how she had felt that she travelled famous and unfamiliar countries when she sat with Miguel over his books and his perceptions. And again she seemed a tourist, again she had held but a postcard of this room which now, through a voyage of possession, she saw in all its vastness and in all of its dimensions.

As if he had understood her new position, and his consequent social elevation, Miguel came for the first time to the front door, and as it stood open, entered without knocking. He placed Milton and Defoe rather timidly on one of the stacks, however, and stood then with his hands in his pockets in an attitude that was at once uneasy, deferential and artificially casual.

"Hi, Miguel," she greeted him easily, and then remembered with a start that this was not perhaps the tone he would expect of her.

"I thought . . ." he shifted his huarachas about on the carpet, "that I'd come and return these books." Then at something of a loss for further conversation, he surveyed the empty shelves with a look that was not really curious, that suggested in fact that he did not notice what had happened. "I finished them," he added.

"Miguel," Millie said kindly, trying to be solemn without being deceptively sad, "I want you to know that this isn't going to make any difference at all about our studying together, about our Saturday mornings. In fact, now that school's out you may come as often as you like."

His face clouded and flashed with brief terror before his lids cached his eyes, and stammering a little he brought out, "The . . . poem isn't going to make any difference?"

"Oh, Miguel!" She had not at all forgotten. The white dove had been all through these days hovering at the freest edge of her mind. She had thought so often of it, in fact, and with such certain pleasure, that it seemed impossible Miguel did not yet know how it laid the seal upon her hopes for him.

"Oh, Miguel, I hadn't forgotten. But this death . . . there's been so much. It was so lovely. You must bring it to me, and we'll go over it together. I can't tell you how . . . I had doubts about your talent sometimes before, but now I'm so certain of you Miguel!"

"But I don't know if I, I don't think I can do it again. I can't, in fact. . . ."

"Nonsense. Never mind. You said that before, and there's plenty of time. It was ... a great comfort to me." Although she had not been in need of comfort, this was something close to what she meant, and she let it stand. Miguel relaxed with a short heavy sigh of relief that only partly satisfied her desire to convince him.

"Can I help?" he asked.

"Yes, if you really want to. I want to take all the books out of those shelves and put them on the other side of the mantel." He immediately went to the shelves she indicated and pulled down an armload. Millie followed him and laid her hands along his jaw.

"Miguel, listen to me. It must seem to you that the poem can't have meant very much. But it's only that a funeral takes more time than it ought to in this world, and you haven't come to see me. I could quote you lines from it now. I will, if you like. I mean this, that it proves to me that there's real talent in you. Great talent, perhaps. I'm not a judge because I've never known a genius. But I've known great poems, and early poems of great men, and your Snow Dove is one of them."

The boy just perceptibly shrank from her caress, and the cheek where her fingers touched it was warm, and touched with damp along the fine brown down.

"You seem feverish, Miguel. Did you sleep well?"

"Yes. I had a dream."

"Oh, I'm sorry."

"No, a good dream. At least not a bad one. Funny."

"What was it like?"

"Well," he rose with hopeful candour from the books he had stacked on the floor, "do you want to hear about it?"

"Of course. Why not?"

He launched straight into it, anxiously, matching his tone with the stride back to the bookcase. "You see, there was a courtroom with a great high pulpit sort of judge's bench. But the judge was a priest. But he was Plato."

"How did you know?" Millie laughed, helping with the books.

"I don't know how." He pondered. "You know these things in dreams."

"Yes, all right, go on."

"And my sister was sitting at a table down below with a big notebook, writing in it—she can't write—and chewing on her hair. She was the—cleric, is it?"

"Clerk."

"Clerk. And my mother was sitting in a chair at the side, on the platform, all slumped and confused looking. She was wearing her wall crucifix stuck in a rag tied around her forehead like an Indian headband. You see? Straight up in front."

"Good heavens!"

"Yes. She was in the witness box there, so he—the judge, the priest, Plato—ought to have been questioning her, but he was questioning me. I was on the floor . . . I don't know where I was."

"Uh-huh."

"And he stood up and held out a book and said I was supposed to solemnly swear to tell the Yes, the whole Yes and nothing but the Yes so help me Glaucon. The book was *Robinson Crusoe*. So I put my hand on it and said I'd do nothing of the sort, and he seemed satisfied and sat down."

"Miguel!"

"Wait. First he said was it or was it not true that Robinson Crusoe knew of the existence of Man Friday because he saw a footprint in the sand which hadn't been there before—the day before."

"What did you say?"

"I said yes."

"Ah-hah!"

"Well, I had to say yes to that. I wasn't going to *lie*."

"And then?"

"Then he said, 'And because he saw the effect, the footprint, he knew that there was of necessity the cause, the man!' 'Yes,' I said. 'In the same way'—he was very quiet and patient, just patient enough to show he thought I was stupid, 'In the same way,' he said, 'as we look about us and perceive the effect, the world, we understand that there is of necessity the cause, God.' My sister was scribbling away furiously. I think she had a colouring book in there."

"And you said yes."

"No! I said in the first place, Robinson Crusoe knew what had caused the footprint because he'd seen feet and footprints before. But say he'd been born on that island, and a . . . wolf, for instance, brought him up, and had chewed off his feet so he went around on his knees. . ." Trotting back and forth to the bookcase, emptying the shelves and stacking the floor, Miguel chattered on as a child chatters who continues to balance his building blocks, having forgotten them in favour of a fairy tale. "Then, I said, he wouldn't have known anything at all about Man Friday."

"Which proves," Millie concluded, "that we don't know anything about the nature of God, since we haven't seen what sort of creature makes this sort of earth."

"Yes!"

"But," she objected, "it doesn't prove anything else—it doesn't prove that there wasn't some sort of cause, or that Crusoe wouldn't have known there was a cause."

"That's just what he said! But don't you see, I had him as good as admitting he couldn't know the nature of God."

"I see."

"Oh, I had him worried. My mother just sat there, hunched over kind of anxious, but not half listening. I think my sister'd stopped chewing her hair."

"Was that the end?"

"No, no. Just the beginning. 'Well,' I said, 'you said that Robinson Crusoe knew there was a cause because he saw a footprint that hadn't been there before. Now, we've never seen chaos, or a universe that hasn't had a world in it.'"

"Even if it had been there all along, Miguel, it would have had to have a cause."

"Nonsense. How do you know? Well, and even if so, you're assuming that. It's not a proof of anything. But it's not important anyway. 'Assuming,' I said, 'that there has to be a cause,

that whatever exists must have a cause, that
the cause exists, then if it exists it has to be an
effect of something else.' Do you follow me?"

"Just barely."

"Well, if the world is the effect of a cause, God,
who exists, then God has to be the effect of a
cause, a Super-god, who exists, who has to be
the effect of a cause, an Ultrasupergod, who
exists, who. . . ."

Forcefully Millie saw again the endless
growing height of ruffle and lock and frond, to
the sky, to the top of the sky, to the ceiling of
heaven which receded, drew away to make
room. . . . "Yes, go on."

"And how do you know where to stop, how can
you stop with God if that's so? Mightn't you just
as well stop with the world?"

"I see."

"Well, he said that it all meant nothing. He
said that it was not a question of a series, but
the difference between perfection and
imperfection, infinity and the finite."

"How did he know that?"

"Exactly, yes, how did he? Oh he knew though
he wasn't on very safe ground. I said that we
have all kinds, all kinds of creators on the earth;
imperfect creators making imperfect creations,

finite creators making finite creations. What right did he—did anybody—have to assume, assuming that the world is imperfect and finite, that its creator is perfect and infinite?"

"You had him."

"I knew it too. 'And besides,' I said—I was pretty tall by this time, I was looking down on to the top of that altar-bench thing, and the top of my sister's dirty hair, and that plastic crucifix on my mother. . . ."

"M-mmm?"

" 'Besides, if God is perfect, what conceivable need could he have to create something, such a muck of a footprint as the world? If he was forever, why would he bother to make up time, or fill the universe with something less perfect, infinitely less perfect if perfect means infinite, than himself?'"

"And what did he say to that?"

Miguel stopped, holding in both hands the two last volumes of the lower shelf, holding them thoughtfully at the oblique same angle as his head, and Millie all unconsciously mirrored his stance with the expectant stillness of her own.

"He said that the world is a bleeding wound, flowing from the side of God."

Slowly Millie fingered the rough page edges of the books she held. "Did you really dream all of that so clearly?" It was an impressed and totally rhetorical question, but unexpectedly Miguel flushed, and abruptly deposited the last books on the stack-crowded floor.

"No," he said with extreme simplicity, "I made it up."

A shadow passed over Miguel, so in keeping with his aspect that it was some seconds before Millie realized that the impression was actual, and that a man in a pale blue shirt, its sleeves rolled to the elbow, was standing in the doorway, kneading the brim of a grey felt hat in powerful fists.

"Good morning, Ma'am," he said.

Millie recognized him with curiosity and pleasure. "Good morning," she said. "May I help you?"

"Well in fact," he said in his soft Texan, funereal tone, "that's what I came to ask you." He ventured a step inside the door, and his foreshortened shadow across the carpet and books accentuated both the width of his shoulders and the delicacy of his head. Miguel stepped out of its path.

"I heard about your . . . your . . . bereavement, and I thought you might be in need of a man's.. of some help."

His excuse, quite plausibly commendable, he managed to make almost ridiculous with the choice of the stilted word and the hungry interest with which he watched Millie Delaney. Miguel displayed a pink tongue tip in the corner of his mouth and compressed his lips with suspicion.

"My name is Karl Ormerod," the man said.

"How do you do. I'm Millie Delaney, as you seem to know, and this is Miguel Laureado."

"Hello, Miguel. I heard you the other day up at the commencement. I thought your poem was very fine."

"Do you like poetry?" Miguel's question was not by way of thanks.

"I like some poetry. I like the poetry I don't dislike. I liked yours fine. You must be proud of him," he added to Millie.

She, torn between the desire to be friendly and the wish not to annoy Miguel, nodded noncommittally.

"Well, if there's anything I could do."

"Yes. To begin with, you could move that bookcase over to where the sideboard is now. I'm rearranging a lot of things."

He grinned at this suggestion, and dropped his hat on the marble table. The gesture seemed to suggest in him too a sensitivity to possession.

"Where d'you want the sideboard? If you guide the back legs over the rug I'll handle the rest of it."

"That's very kind of you."

"I guess there's more books here than the Houston library. Do you store them in the basement too, like they do?"

"This house hasn't got a basement," Miguel said.

"They belonged to my father. At least, they belonged to an uncle of my father's. They came to me very early, though. My father wasn't much of a reader—except of bank statements."

"My father owns a bank," Karl too eagerly supplied a common link. "In Houston, Texas. A great grey box of a place."

"My father's dead," Miguel intervened aggressively. Millie turned on him with quiet reproach. "So is mine, Miguel."

"Well," the boy said with an elaborate shrug, "if you can get along without me, I think I'd better get back to my reading. There's a lot of studying to be done . . ." he stooped to the two largest volumes in sight, Dante and St. Augustine.

"Really, Miguel. If I were you, I'd start the vacation on Dickens." She smiled at him with private significance. "How about *Great Expectations*?"

He accepted the book, but retained his hold on the others, and carried all three with him to the door. "I'll see you tomorrow at the usual time."

"All right then. Good-bye, Miguel."

"So long, Miguel. Adios."

They watched him go with a slight rebirth of the original embarrassment.

"I'm afraid I've made him jealous. I'm sorry."

"Oh, it's nothing. He's a little sullen sometimes, but he gets over it quickly. It's an occupational hazard of talent I expect. Do you really mind helping?"

"What do you think I came for?"

"I'm not certain."

"Well, there's something in that. Let's get to it."

The sideboard had settled into its place with the weight of thirty years, and at their first efforts it tilted and shot out its centre drawer in a clatter of silver serving spoons and Geegee's harmonica.

"Oh, hell, I'm sorry."

"Never mind. Maybe we'd better take everything out of it."

They did so, and presently stood in a wide confusion of pitchers and forks, clocks and crystal mixing bowls, as in a litter of mutual prospective domesticity. Then, of course, they discovered that they had hemmed in the sideboard with the semi-circle of fragile debris, and collapsed stupidly on the sofa, laughing at each other's inefficiency.

"Oh, they teach us engineering at the quarry, all right."

"You lived in Houston, did you?"

"Mmm; as long as I could. I worked in my father's bank until I felt so, oh, out of touch, somehow, I had to get out."

"So you came to Sintiempo!"

"Well, I don't guess that's much of an adventure to you."

"Not much."

"You were born here?"

"In this house. I've been as far as Athens in my books. But Houston seems another planet altogether."

"I guess so. But it's the same earth, you can take my word for it. I think you can probably go stir crazy in a teller's cage faster than Alcatraz."

"Was it so bad?"

"It was for me. No, it wasn't so bad. People were terrifically damn polite. But I was never certain they weren't being polite to the manager's son."

"Of course."

"And then the place itself. People—you got to know their faces in little stripes between the bars, and the way they sounded when they said 'in fives please', or something like that. And a little steam radiator wheezing away about the level of your knees. And marking down numbers—marking time. I don't know. It was a good job they tell me. But the ceiling was too low. There wasn't ... I felt as if there wasn't room to grow. Do you know what I mean?"

He watched Millie a little warily, as if afraid she might facetiously remind him of his height. But she was nodding solemnly, frowning at a dust smudge on her trouser knee, which she rubbed with a slow, slender finger.

"Yes, I do," she said. "I understand exactly. Would you like to stay to lunch?"

XIV

He stayed to lunch, and after that he stayed to dinner, which they improvised of tinned spaghetti and tomato soup, and after that he would have stayed to breakfast if he had seen in Millie's behaviour anything that might have been interpreted as an invitation.

He did not, and yet she was not at all the girl that he had feared. She seemed all made of the stuff of twirling cartwheels he had seen in her patio, and bearing not the remotest resemblance, or only quaint endearing flashes of resemblance, to the community schoolteacher Sintiempo had praised. There was a freedom about her that had the air of novelty; she was candid with a graceful awkwardness as if candour were her nature but not her habitual pose. She threw back her head and laughed toward the ceiling when she laughed, and he told her that it was the laugh of a swashbuckling pirate. This was a rare flight of fancy on Karl's part, at which he was himself surprised and pleased, and she, pleased and suddenly quite shy. At this he was rather more surprised and only slightly less pleased, and concluded that she was very deep, though not at all deceptive.

He found himself liking, in fact, a great deal that he would not in theory have praised. He, who preferred as a rule the softest parts of the roundest women, liked the spare line of her back arched over the stove, drawing as it did the white shirt taut across her spine. He had a simple desire to run his hand along this line, and he simply did so, at which she shied away spilling tomato broth, and became very distant for a full ten minutes. This too he liked.

He liked her eager quoting of poetry snatches, when he faltered to define a difficult feeling in simple words, as if she could not help herself, but could borrow words that would. He liked the intense way she questioned him about Houston, about the University of Texas through which he had dawdled and scraped, about the reasons for his leaving. He would have for his own part told her that he deserted the recruiting office, but for his inability to predict what line she would take on so controversial an ideal. So, at her insistence, he tried to embellish dissatisfaction of the universe with which, as a matter of fact, he was very little dissatisfied. There is nothing more genuine than the impulse to share with a new and beautiful person one's own lack of purpose, and nothing which so fades that sense to the innocuous background as a new and beautiful person wishing to share. He avoided the subject of senseless war, partly from the fear that her knowledge of politics would be more comprehensive and convincing than his own, partly to avoid the confession it might prompt. Instead, he described the bank in fuller detail, recounted his two week flight as if it had been taken on a swayback mare for the mere adventure of it, imitated the nasal drawl and the officious folksiness of Vernon Smee's, "M'boy, hamstrung, tied, absolutely". He had never employed such art to please a woman, had believed that all the studied parts of charm belonged to them, and that his own office was a silent and ready acceptance. Now, to an extent of which he would not have believed himself capable, he found himself supplying the flirtatious insinuations which Millie Delaney wholly lacked. This too he liked.

"Then how long did you stay in Railton?"

"Eight months, eight whole months, October to May."

"What did you leave for?"

"Oh, well, it was the same thing, you know. Statements and accounts. I might never have left home."

"You must feel very strongly about it."

"Not necessarily. I feel very strongly about the desert."

"In what way?"

"What do you mean? I love the desert, that's all. I wanted to be out in it."

"Really do you?"

"Do I what?"

"Love the desert?"

"You sound like it's a new idea. Don't you?"

"Oh, no, I don't think so. Well, I like . . . you know, the weather in October and April, and yuccas, and some of the trees, and oh, baby spine toads."

"That's my name!"

"What's your name?"

"Toad. That's what they call me at the quarry."

"Why ever?"

"From 'Todo'. I don't know why; they get a kick out of it."

"It doesn't fit you at all."

"But it sticks."

"Well then, I guess I like big toads too." This was evidently very bold for her. They were sitting for supper at the marble table in the living room, having decided that the dining table was too big and the kitchen too small. The sideboard was now neatly in the nook of the stairwell, and every book in place on the south wall, starting with Sophocles at the upper left and ending at the lower right with Lewis Carroll. Millie was not eating much; she speared the spaghetti and coiled it into little spirals about her fork, then lifted her fork and attacked in another place without raising it to her mouth.

"Thank you," he said with a steady open gaze, searching her face for signs.

And there was a sign; a kind of expectant patience in her returning smile, abandoned but serene. What Karl had done to win the confidence of this apparently solitary girl—apparently solitary by choice—he could not guess. She certainly did not seem to be suffering from the death of her guardian. But he thought more of himself for it, and he felt a protective tenderness for Millie that he usually squandered vaguely on the victims of wars, on beautiful and helpless animals toward whom he was helpless. Yet clearly she was not one of those.

"Do you think you could make me love the desert?" she challenged with a smile.

"Oh, well! Do you think you could make me love your books?"

In that many words they agreed to spend their time together. They planned that Millie should meet him next day with a picnic lunch at noon at the quarry, and Karl, reassured by her promise, took his leave at the respectable hour of ten o'clock. She followed him to the door, carrying his hat, and when Karl turned he was conscious with a sinking tremor of the brush of his elbow on her breast. He had expected, when he kissed her, a prelude or a pretence of resistance, so her simple yielding caught him somewhat off guard. He pressed the advantage too far, became conscious himself of the cruelty of his fingers' grip on her shoulders and the painful pressure of his kiss, so that she ended by stiffening, and pushing him at last away. It was an inversion of the proper process, and extraordinarily unsatisfactory. Disappointed and a little anxious, he put all the deep respectfulness of romance into an "Oh, Millie", and quickly left.

XV

When she woke again in the sun square of the double bed, it was with the feverishness of fitful sleep. The slightest movement made her chest contract and her face flush as if from physical illness; her arms, locked around the pillow, trembled in the sunlight; and through her mind turned a series of pictures like bright vignettes, Karl smiling, Karl solemn, Karl puzzled, Karl rolling a cigarette. She lay for a long time with a look that was like a child's eager terror, more astonished in retrospect than she had been at the time, at the completeness with which she had accepted him into her life. Then for a long time she lay wondering what she had had on all the other mornings of her life to think about, and but for Miguel, could remember nothing.

When she rose she found herself unsteady on her feet, and laughed a little at the semblance of convalescence in her careful walk. She put on the green skirt with a bright red sash, and a ribbon in her hair; and grinning foolishly she wandered past the palms to town with a market basket on her arm. Her breast burned with the brush of Karl's elbow. People she met nodded

admiringly at her cheerfulness, which seemed
to them a little strained, but brave. Outside the
drugstore she passed a flat-nosed, shock-haired
youth waiting by an empty pram, and greeting
him she remembered with sudden embarrassment that he had kissed her once. At
recess on the high school playing field; a wet
fumbling kiss that had missed its mark by some
length of nose, and landed high on an averted
cheek without the power to frighten or excite.
With obscure mischievousness she stopped and
inquired after the wife, the baby, and the ranch;
deplored the weather and accepted his
condolences, wished him good morning and
passed on to Gallencamp's. She placed her
extravagant order and carried home with her,
humming, a heavy load of picnic. stuff. The door
was ajar, and Miguel had come and gone,
leaving *Great Expectations* by way of a calling
card. She was touched by the number of hours
he must have spent reading, reproached herself
with forgetting, and then yielding again to the
fullness of new sensations, condoned herself and
promised to make it up to him later.

At eleven thirty, the basket again on her arm,
a daisy tucked at the side of her sash, her legs
still uncertain with a trembling ache, she

started for Lenajidak peak across the valley. The perfect stillness of the desert mocked her agitation. Here and there a lizard sunned, its belly flat to the rock, lazily watching her pass. She circled to the left of the Mexican village, dry and sleeping, toward the mountain that droned with the steadiness of its drills like a crouched and static insect. The only wind was of her own making, so the mesquite trees, as if catching her mood, shivered as she passed, shed a few grey pinpoint leaves from their supple needles, and were still again. The shadow she cast was scarcely bigger than her steps, and passed smoothly over shining quartzite flakes that predicted the nearness of marble. The quarry noon whistle broke with such brief vertical shrieking that it seemed to ascend and disappear straight into the sun, mounted in the perfect centre of the pale blue bowl. The drilling died with the shrill signal, and such perfect stillness followed that it seemed her heart alone yet sounded in the universe, the steady witness of heat and effort and love.

She climbed a mound to the east of the quarry and saw the dark workers ranging themselves with bags and lunch baskets in the straight, single significant shade of the smokestack, as if on a long low bench. But the one, pale as the mountain and empty-handed, detached himself with a wave to them and started in her direction, out of her sight at a walk over a hill, into it again at a run, and then perspiring and breathless, he stopped short and put a hand to his slender jaw, and laughed anxiously, "I'm dirty".

For answer she ran to him and flung her arms around his waist, burying her face in his shirt front. "I don't know what's the matter with me. . . I . . ." and the stillness fell again, but with his heart answering her own. She broke from his kiss catching for breath and brushing a tear that mingled with the fine damp on the down of her cheek. "The . . . its . . . the desert is so lovely!"

"So lovely you're lovely I love you," he chorused her words without a pause, and caught her again with a cry, after which they fell laughing on the smooth slope of rock and lay with their hands clasped close between their faces, wonderingly smiling, shaking their heads foolishly at the inadequacy of words.

They found a mesquite's scant shade for their picnic, spread the sandwich and fruit profusion grandly out, and then ignored it, not noticing that they did not eat. They talked in that rare stumbling eagerness of unlike minds, the ideas so tumbling from each other, so complimenting each other, so exactly converging in momentary flashes of feeling only to diverge for stretches of narrative, that Millie once interrupted herself interrupting him to boast that they had so much to say to each other they should never succeed to a period.

He talked about his childhood, as of an object long fallen into disuse. He would describe a Sunday treat that had taken him from the arid polish of the young desert city into the mountain farmlands or the wind-rounded boulders of sandstone hills. He would, haltingly, salting his sentence with quick demands for affirmation of understanding—"do you see?" "you know?" "you get what I mean?"—describe his sense of escape on a pony ride in the level sands; or a rock search in the open, unconcealing hills. And she would jump at his suggestion; adopt the sentiment; recognize it as her own, and match him volume for farm, poem for hill, answering him with her own escape from the city of her home to the desert of her books. They established a habit, new to them both, which was to last with them as long as they lasted together; he of declaring, she of affirming and embellishing, seeming perfectly to comprehend. He had a talent for telling an incident, all simply, but with such genuine enjoyment or emotion himself that it was impossible not to share, impossible not to think him funny when he laughed, touching when he himself was moved. And though the things of which he spoke, down to the domestic habits of the western poor and the names of spine-petaled flowers, were the things of which her confining life had been only too full, he was to her a window out of the mountains. The very newness of him set in the newness of her freedom made him seem like some wonderful pale-bound book, taking the familiar and making it strange; so that the convergence of their backgrounds seemed rather a link than a weight.

He too was new to this part of romance. All he wanted and expected of a woman he had yet to have of this one; but though he was impatient, he was not bored. He had so often parroted the formula of devotion, not as genuine but as the means to a goal genuinely desired, that he held back from it now, restrained himself even from saying again that he loved her, as he restrained himself physically from frightening her. She was interested in his life; he became interested in it too. He tried to make something concrete and important of his desire for escape, which was a desire for peace; she described her own, which was a desire for adventure, and he accepted it as his. So well did they seem to understand each other that neither once realized that he spoke of nature, and she of art.

He stood at last, reluctantly, and pulled her lightly from the rock.

"An hombre's got to earn his bread."

She laughed at his language as if he had affected it to amuse her, and buried her face again where it reached him, stomach high. "Will you come for dinner?"

"May I?"

"You may not not."

"Yes, Ma'am." And they stood for a moment longer looking out over the desert plain away from Sintiempo, breathing waves of heat for its clear hundred miles.

"Do you know," he asked, "that from here you can see seven counties and four states and two countries?"

She knew it very well. It was a boast from which no one in Sintiempo, not even her ladylike mother, had ever been free. It had seemed to her at times the only value they could find in their town or their lives or themselves. But Karl in his immensity made it immense for her. So much emptiness, so much starved life, such endless wandering of the railroad tracks; and Railton set like a pasteboard toy at its plywood edge. Karl was stretching his eyesight with a look like wonder, and she loved him suddenly for everything she failed to love. She denied him, however, "No, that is space, not size. There is more size in Sintiempo than that." She pulled away gently toward the untouched picnic.

Karl went back to the quarry feeling rebuffed at the moment of perfection, and did not realize that even as she folded the food in the cloth she had forgotten her words and was measuring with dismay the hours until dinner-time. It might not always be so, but now her absorption in him was impermeable to the point of callousness. She walked back more slowly, intensely happy, intensely full. Her life had changed direction, had found direction, and it seemed as if, whatever she had been searching, had been circling and seeing dimly, she now strode toward surely and in a straight, bright line. She tried to read and could not. She set the table at three o'clock and covered it with flowers which were dead by four. She replaced them with others in a shallow platter of water, and the room was filled with the acrid sweet perfume of prickly-pear and saguaro blooms. She took a long bath, sliding her soap covered hands the length of her slippery self, and feeling for the first time that she was beautiful, and worthy of presenting. She had not, like the girls she had known and Karl had known, toyed early with passion and given in, fumbling, by degrees, to fumbling young men. And this Karl knew, so that when he came, and when he stayed, he disbelieved at first her total acceptance of him, and when he believed it, he misunderstood it. He was delighted that she did not hold back from him, but he did not understand that he must. He had great tenderness for her, but tenderness in him expressed itself in yet greater openness and abandon. She offered herself to be taught, and he took her, not wishing to be cruel, not knowing to be gentle, and it was terrible to her. He remembered his own first experience, at fifteen, jeered into the sultry Houston whorehouse by his older friends; his horror and his sense of failure and his two years of subsequent celibacy. But he thought of it only in a thrill of contrast to this deep softness and soul-whole participation. He knew that she was physically hurt, and physically unfulfilled, but this he knew natural, and of other hurts and unfulfilments he had no conception. He wanted to please her as she in her yielding innocence had pleased him, and so forced himself on her again, toward morning, and she was less yielding, seeing her own body as a brash hard yellow in the sunlight and wishing it were cooler so that she could cover herself with the white sheet. Karl's lip curled slightly with passion, like the suggestion of a sneer, and she closed her eyes and yielded herself this time to endure, feeling nothing but grotesqueness and her own consummation by all the unrealizing ugliness of life.

So that later, at breakfast, Karl sitting beautiful in spent strength and smiling uncontrollably, she covered again in cool white cotton and handling implements she knew how to control, her relief overwhelmed her, and spilled itself in tears very much like tears of joy. He came to her, concerned and soft, and she said, "So happy," which seemed to her instantly the truth, and they stood rocking together back and forth while the eggs spluttered and went brown at the edges. She broke away from him with a cry of a laugh and scraped them from the pan. But he wouldn't have it, locked his arms around her shoulders and brushed his nose in her hair.

"I suppose you realize, Miss Delaney," he said in his soft drawling way, "that I had the pleasure of making your acquaintance nearly forty-eight hours ago."

She was shocked and proud at once. She had been proud of the speed of her surety, but her surety was less now, and her pride faltered. She turned back to him and giggled into his breast. "Isn't it silly," she said, and was not sure what she meant. He praised the eggs, which were burnt and cold when they ate them, and she was immensely proud. They talked again in the stumbling eager way, and she, anxious to please him and to reassure herself, kept jumping from the table to the bookcase, to read him what he meant. He loved her high, flowing, almost childishly rhythmical voice, and a muscle that tensed over her right eyebrow, and the anxiousness with which she looked up from a passage to his face; waiting for approval; so he would say, "That's lovely, that's beautiful," and she gloried in his intent patience, his willingness to let her read on and again.

When he left for the quarry, too late and hurriedly, she thought she couldn't bear it, and made mock scenes of a horror of desertion, which delighted him, so that they parted again in excited laughter.

It was the same for nearly two weeks, or nearly the same. He ran from the quarry at six, like a husband, and like a wife she greeted him in an apron, open eyed, expectant, as if waiting for a gift. He would take a bath, and come down to dinner fresh-shaven, smelling of soap, with anecdotes carefully salvaged from the day's work. He was interested in the quarry, and believed that a new road and modern machinery would make it pay. She sat with him over catalogues and transportation rate schedules and pages of figures, uninterested herself but proud of him because he had an interest. He had even, one day, an idea for making Sintiempo into an artist's colony—"If the sculptors would come to the marble, don't you see, they could have it almost at cost." She thought it absurd; and half knew that he had suggested it only to please her, but she grabbed at it as a confirmation of artistic feeling in him, and pretended to think it possible.

She would sit curled in his lap on the sofa after dinner, while he smoked and she drank black coffee, and she would dart her head to his face when he raised the cigarette, pretending jealousy of it. She was always desolate to see him go, always glad to tears when he came, so that there was nothing in her which did not speak of total love. Sometimes he carried her up the stairs, rocking her like a loved animal, and she would be soft and content with expectancy, thinking, this time it will be gentle and beautiful. Sometimes they would go early to bed and lie still for an hour, talking in low tones and watching the yucca bend to the window pane, and the stars growing as the sky deepened to a black violet. And then she would lie, her shoulder tucked under his arm, her ankle hung lightly over his calf, supremely happy. But always, her very gentleness roused in him the passion that did not know not to be cruel. And even in her sleep she would wait for morning once again, when he would have to go off to the quarry, and she could nestle against him for good-bye, without being crushed and torn by him.

One night they took a walk on the dark desert and gathered warm glittering pebbles of

quartzite from the hillside; and finding a fresh-
blown dune, made patterns with their footsteps,
crossing and recrossing and circling and coming
together; toe to toe. They were immensely proud
of themselves. She took off her shoes and danced
in the sand, danced on her toes; taunting him,
in utmost candour. But that night, tired and
happy, happy and afraid of spoiling her
happiness, she refused him, kissed him with a
look that asked to be forgiven, and turned away.
He could not believe it. For the third time, at the
very height of their unity, she had closed herself
off from him, deceivingly, like a desert animal.
She took such obvious joy in everything short of
their love making, in his caress, in her own
tempting, in their very nakedness, that he could
not conceive there was any terror or disgust or
shrinking hidden in her. He was hurt, and
hardened, and at breakfast they quarrelled,
attaching bitter superlatives to minor
complaints, calling forever down on the
moment's irritation. He accused her of
insensitivity, and she burst forth with a ragged
gasp of a laugh, and clattered the skillet
carelessly. She set his eggs before him with a
look of martyrdom like thunder, and he
tightened his small beautiful mouth in the

hatred of incomprehension. She clattered the pans again, recklessly took a glass jar from the cupboard, and with her tensed back to him tilted the skillet clanking to the lip of the jar. The jar broke from the heat; the boiling fat ran over her fingers and poured scalding on her bare foot. He was at her side with a cry of his own pain, holding her anxiously; kissing her tears, inspecting the injured hand, and it was all right once more. "Thank God for it," she said.

She gave herself up to him again. Afraid of his anger and ashamed of her own failure, she began to pretend that she, too, reached her climax and was happy with him. He exulted. But she faded a little from day to day. In the second week she complained often of tiredness. She let the flowers stay wilted on the table some days. She read again when he was at the quarry, but she read less to him, and was less satisfied with his patient listening. He always said that what she read was beautiful, but soon she wanted more, wanted him to say in what way it was beautiful, or why, or even to say that it was not. She began to catch herself flinching when he used a slang word, shrinking when he used an obscene word which she knew she made beautiful to him. She was ashamed of these things; they seemed an inadequacy of love in herself, and being ashamed, she resented them more.

Strangely, in the town at this time, little was said of Millie Delaney. The gossip subsided in direct inverse proportion to the obviousness of the affair. There was the usual acceptance of Millie's motives, and among the women a kind of soft satisfaction, almost relief, that Millie Delaney was in love. If a townswoman broached indiscreetly or with inadequate respect the subject of Millie's young man, she was likely to be answered with an excess of magnanimous pleasure, "Yes, isn't it grand? I'm so happy for the child." Rebuffed, the gossiper would use the same technique on her less discreet neighbour, so that the benevolence spread faster than the scandal.

Then, situated as it was between the quarry and the town, no one need see or know for sure at what hour young Toad came to Millie's house, or when he left. The life of the Mexican village was wholly detached from that of Sintiempo; no one need find out that he did not sleep at the quarry. The only person who went by morning from the town to the quarry was the foreman, Joshua Pitz, a wizened and weasel-eyed man who usually arrived at the drilling plot before dawn. If he noticed from which direction Toad came, he might once have given him a sidewise wink, but of this even Karl himself was not certain. Aside from that, there was no one forced to see anything he did not care to, no one who could not, if he chose, make the most romance and the least scandal of the love of the big blond man and the small dark girl.

No one except, of course, for the grocery boy, who occasionally in early morning passed the lover on the road between the Mexican village and the Delaney house, and walked on staring at his stubbing toes with a look of hatred that was more like fear; and a look of fear like shame.

The Moon

XVI

"You're a fool, Millie. You're crazy out of your mind," glowering from the kitchen step, Toad crushed his grey stetson between his fists. "You got a world of ideas in your head don't have anything more to do with the real world than…" It was not the first time metaphor had failed him. The fingers clenching at the hat strained muscles the length of his thick arm. "I don't understand you," and in spite of the attempted sneer, the stumble of his words proved that this was true.

"I know. Please. . . . Please don't try."

"You're not human!"

"I'm not an animal," Millie said, which did not have anything at all to do with what she meant.

"You're not natural; you're not alive!" One side of Toad's upper lip curled savagely, and Millie winced, there! That's exactly the way he looks when he's making love. Toad was almost too tall for the door, and his head came so close to the arch that she had the sudden impression he was wedged there. She raised one hand as if to push him, but lowered it at once and said, "Please go". His workshirt sleeves were rolled to the shoulder, and she watched the veins so delicately tensing with his muscles. Such beautiful skin, better fit for posing in marble than for drilling it. She wilfully remembered his whole skin, paler than the quarry sun should have allowed, strong and polished like marble, beautiful. . . . The strangest part, she thought, is that I could want him again if I made up my will to it.

"Please go, Toad."

"You're not alive," he said again, and as his voice faltered, "you're crazy loco!"

Her instant revulsion at his illogic and his slang was replaced the next instant with renewed weariness. How is it possible, she thought, sick of herself and of being sick of herself, to hate so much for such little reasons. And how could I have loved so much, and for what reasons at all?

"Listen, Millie," his voice softened, and he took her elbow. "There's nothing strange about you feeling guilty. It's just the ideas you got, being brought up how you were. You can't get over that all at once."

"It isn't that." In fact, Millie had tried very hard to feel guilty, to see the facts of the affair through the other women's eyes, but she remembered instead the mouth of Mrs. Erlintuck chewing on a rumour as she spat it out, and Mrs. Wesch gaping to receive it, biting down on it, her jowls settling with enormous finality into her double chin. Oh, it was so much simpler not to sin than to feel sincerely guilty.

"Millie, look at me. If you can look me in the eye and say, 'I don't love you,' I'll go."

"I do not love you," she said, but though this was in fact the case, she couldn't look at him to say it, and he would not have believed her at any rate.

"I said look at me! Millie, you know you don't mean that."

"Toad," she said, and the anguish in her face was more than she felt, she knew, "I do mean that I want you to go. Please don't try to understand it." She searched herself for some fragment of the struggle she should be feeling; if she could make it mysterious, perhaps he could salvage something bittersweet and bearable. But her words were only tired. "If I knew any way to explain, I would have done so before this. Please . . . just go, and don't come back."

He leaned to her, tightening his grip, and one white lock fell wet on his forehead. "Have you forgotten everything we had together, Millie?"

"Yes," she said.

Toad's lip curled back again, "You'll get hurt someday, Millie Delaney, and find out what feeling is. You don't know anything more about living now than. . . ."

He seemed about to kiss her, but thought better of it and wheeled out the door. At the edge of the porch he turned and shouted brutally, "But if you ever want to learn about it, you can find me at the quarry!" And then as if aware that his words did not suit his tone, he rubbed a hand across his mouth and walked rapidly away. Millie closed the door without watching him go.

She leaned against it, locking it behind her back. Miguel's poem ran in her mind in broken phrases. . . .

> *alone, alone,*
> *Alone and without master*
> *Without a love alone*
> *And in a foreign town . . .*

Out of the kitchen window she could see the back road stretch toward town, crack-dry, but seeming to steam in the mirage of June sun. The small brown boy was not on it yet. Perhaps he would be late, and without that one loved thing in all the landscape of Sintiempo, the sun lost itself in the road ruts, withered over fields of weeds, and ricocheted from lids of garbage cans and broken bottles. It cast a square spotlight on Millie Delaney's kitchen floor, and she put a foot in it, watching the dust settle, settle, settling.

Once in class, in April, Miguel had abruptly thrust a hand up, "Miss Delaney!"

"Yes, Miguel."

His gravity never altered; he gave himself away only by slipping thickly into the old Mexican accent. "Miss Delaney, you would please ex-plain why the round sun turns square when it comes into the room on the floor."

Sternly: "You will please investigate for yourself, and make a report on it tomorrow." Then Miguel came next day bearing the black notebook, which he called an encyclopedia, and stood stiffly before the class, reading from it a series of metaphors for the most part disconnected and far-fetched ("the window is a jello mould that turns out trembling sun-shapes on the floor"), but so startling for Miguel's fourteen years, that Millie's mind set up a descant to his reading, "such promise, promise, promise".

. . . Promise, promise. She took her foot from the sun-square and watched the road again. What promise had she now to give Miguel? The sun shrivelling Sintiempo's weeds outside, and inside the dust forever settling. Oh, Miguel, before you, only the books told me that there was some untouched promise of beauty. But you felt it too, and I was so sure. I am so tired.

It was without any particular resolve that Millie closed the kitchen shutter, and certainly without any sense of a permanent isolation. But when it was done she was drawn to the light on the dining-room carpet, and she blocked the sun from that room too. From a side window she saw Lenajidak and the quarry, the peak where she and Toad had spent an afternoon. She shut them out. She quickly climbed the steps to shut them from the second floor, and her heart and footsteps pounding down again, she locked the doors and pulled the last shutters to. "Now . . . now I have no window but a mirror."

She laid her forearms on the mantelpiece and watched her world's reflection; fringed lampshades from another era, a tapestry piano shawl, a rocker whose leather seat still held the shape of the ancient buttocks it had borne until two weeks ago. Like the books, thought Millie, nothing here was made after 1901, except myself, and I am growing old.

I am growing old, she thought, not in one swift second's fraction, as one would really register dismay at the advancing years, but drawling it through her mind for the full length of Mrs. Angleberger's voice; I am growing . . . old. She searched her face for lines, but there was only her black hair falling, not beautiful, but soft; slight bones; a nose as gently beaked as a small bird's beak. "Ugly nose, Millie Delaney," she observed without conviction, "Milton Ellis Delaney, aged twenty-three."

Her eyes held her until the whole reflection swam and faded but for the little universe of her iris. It had been this way sometimes as a little girl; she watched her face until it was neither

her face nor another face, but Face, and she had said, neither quite believing it nor caring, "That is me. That is *me*." This is now, Millie thought, but her face faded around the fulcrum of her eyes, and she seemed to know everything that she was yet to learn; she seemed to see her life laid out in the foreknown pattern of a life, through which she must proceed, attached by the second-hand of days to the flyspeck of herself.

Wrapped in the same sense of the unreal, Millie covered the date on the calendar beside her with the tip of her little finger. June 28, 1943; a fragment of infinity, with a name and number, like herself. Try to imagine infinity; forever, to the end of time, but time endless, on, on . . . as far as you can imagine seeing, but beyond imagining, and on, on . . . and drop into the space of that Millie Ellie Delaney, aged twenty-three. What difference does it make? June 28, 1943. What does it signify?

"It signifies," wryly Millie orated toward a reflection in sudden focus, "that you are in no little danger of being pregnant."

And because the words did not sound as ridiculous as she had intended, she turned from

the mirror and walked, reaching, to the
bookcase.

XVII

In the morning his mother was sick on the floor. To clean a dirt floor is a contradiction in terms; Miguel did his best with a newspaper and propped the door open with a shoe, almost new, which had arrived in one of the Sintiempo Presbyterian Christmas Charity Baskets without a mate. He took two slices from a drying grocery loaf and handed one to his sister. From the cot his mother moaned softly, asking forgiveness and pity.

" 'Ria, how old are you?" Miguel asked. The girl dug three finger-nails into the slice and held up seven fingers.

"No. Tell me! Aloud." Maria pulled a lock of coarse black hair straight over the top of her head and stuck it in her mouth. Miguel brushed it away. "Look at me, watch my lips. Say: Miguel, I am seven years old."

'Ria wadded half the bread in her fist, and shoved it in her mouth. She chewed deliberately three or four times, and then, begrudgingly "Ssseven".

"*Por dios*!" Miguel swung her around and sat her on the edge of his mother's bed. "Good, 'Ria! Listen to me. You will stay with mamacita today, all day, and I will bring you seven copper moons when I come home." She flung herself down beside her mother and looked up at him sideways through her hair. "Penniesss?" She guessed.

From the open door, the sun slanting from just past dawn caught at the grey in his mother's hair, which, straight and long, strayed across her cheeks like 'Ria's. Señora Laureado rolled her eyes weakly and smiled with limp melodrama.

"Pennies," Miguel promised his sister, "and I will shine them on the blanket till they are bright as moons, and hang them in your hair. You will stay?"

Maria nodded her consent and buried her face in the quilt. "Say 'promise', 'Ria." But she wouldn't look at him again, and stepping into his huarachas, he reached for Miss Delaney's copy of Augustine's *Confessions*, to return it. "*Hasta la noche, mamacita.* I will go the first thing to Mrs. Angleberger, and I will be home early."

Squinting fiercely, he sprinted the road toward Anglebergers', to tell them in the briefest, firmest terms he could assemble, that Señora Laureado could not come to clean today. If he walked and ran alternate blocks, he would not be more than an hour late to Gallencamp's, and if he hurried the first deliveries, he should be at Miss Delaney's by lunchtime. When he got to a crossroad he slowed to a walk and, gravely, absently began to sing.

> *Soy sola, sola*
> *Sola y sin dueño;*
> *Solita sin amores*
> *Y en pueblo ajeño.*

There is a kind of happiness, structured on sand of guilt, that will topple at the slightest gesture, and must be rebuilt once for every finger levelled at it. That his mother was ill, that his sister could not be trusted to stay with her, that Mr. Gallencamp would lecture him for tardiness—these things had held his mind, but had not shaken the joy that had filled him since December, when Miss Delaney had begun to make him know that he was not merely different, but better. (Oh, Miss Delaney had not used those words, but it was impossible not to think in terms of them.) Now, intent on composing his speech for Mrs. Angleberger, he was first aware only of a vague uneasiness at the tune, a trembling deeper than it should have set up in him. But suddenly he stopped and coloured, looked furtively around, though the lots were so level and bare that he would surely have known if anyone was in sight, and then, more rapidly, resumed his walk. The song was an ancient Spanish lullaby, about a white dove. A fair translation of the verse he had just so indiscreetly divulged to the Sintiempo weeds might go something like:

> *I am alone, alone,*
> *Alone and without master;*
> *Without a love alone,*
> *And in a foreign town.*

XVIII

There was in Sintiempo in late June a considerable increase of unpublished marital affection. In the following April the *Sintiempo Sun* was to feature a front-page article entitled "Stork Strikes Home/At Crowded Clinic", and the town's name even made its way on to the wires of the state news service, which had not happened since the founding of the quarry, by virtue of its population, 564, and its two-week birth record, 37. Mothers in succeeding years made much affectionate ado about the coincidence of birthdays in late April. No one of any reasonable, functioning sentimentality entirely escaped the aura. Being a town unused to spring, it habitually grabbed for its romance at the engagement of the baker's daughter and the grocer's son, but this was something rather more. It was the foreigner and the princess, it was the orphan and the prince, it was the alpha and the omega.

Duncan shaved. He wrapped the strop around his knuckles and snapped it taut with a great Whap! and whet his razor. He liked the sound.

He did it again with great vehemence and pulled the strop screw out of the wall. He cursed and knuckled the dangling end between his knees and whet again, and cut his hand. He decided to grow a beard. He squinted at his sleep-puffed face to imagine the beard, a goatee would not be bad, add length to the face, or a short stiff all over round one, rather Russian looking perhaps. Duncan had heard of Russia. Then abruptly he put his forefingers on his lower lids and gave a downward tug, exposing the red-veined whites, and stared at himself with fierce vertical solemnity.

"Never do that again," he commanded aloud in a voice of self-important resolution. "Never, never do that again." He was apt to feel rather underfoot in the summer-time.

He wrapped his cut in a pale green guest towel and sloughed back into his bedroom. Lena was sitting up in bed, wearing a brown feather bedjacket which smelled faintly of camphor and mothballs. She had taken her curlers out, but had not yet combed her hair, which sprang into tight straw coils, like Japanese finger tortures.

"Can't see", Duncan said hostilely, holding his hands behind his back, "as a woman with oily skin ought to cream it up some extra."

All glistening Lena snuggled down into the bed-jacket and broke into her company coo. "Hoooc, Dunkikins, I've told you, if you cream your face the natural oil glands don't work so hard. Honestly."

"Tummyrot." Duncan said.

"Did you put on the coffee now?"

"I cut my hand."

"Lordy, let me see." She angled out of bed and walked around behind him, since he wouldn't offer her his hand. "Duncan," she pouted, "my towel."

Duncan pushed past her and into the hall. He went to the kitchen and emptied a pot full of grounds into the sink. "Honestly," he mumbled in a falsetto, "it's good for the plumbing, coffee grounds." He twisted the water on and watched it swirl around the damp mound, eroding it from the outer edge. He tried to calculate the number of particles sliding over the drain. How many grounds in a pot of coffee? He thought of his first wife, her hair the rich colour of coffee grounds in a cascade on the pillow. "A veritable cascade," he said, and sighed. Empty sink now. He unwrapped his hand and held it under the cold tap. It had stopped bleeding. "Damn Nation," he pronounced without emotion.

Duncan liked his coffee light, thick; strong and three quarters cream. Millie Delaney had told him that the French made their coffee with hot milk. Damn good idea, that. Make a fortune with it in America. His forehead folded slightly in the intensity of invention, Duncan took a pint of cream from the refrigerator and emptied it into the percolator. He filled the tin cup with fresh grounds and set it on the gas. Then he propped the door open and squatted breathily on the porch, trying not to think of the night before. "Never do that again," he said once more with feeling, and added wickedly, "Go elsewhere." This assertion seemed to calm him, and for several minutes he squatted watching the grass click back and forth with the passing of unseen insects.

Intent, it was several seconds before he identified the sound, and several more before he reached the stove, by which time it was unnecessary anyway because the fire was out. The boiling cream crusted the coffee spout and the stove and oozed over the edge in a veritable cascade, making a free form, rather attractive in shape, on the linoleum. Duncan put his foot in it reaching for the gas, and stopped to take off his slipper.

"Dunki," Lena's coo came insinuatingly nearer. He saw her big toe on the doorsill, square under lavender crêpe embroidery.

"Lordy," she said, with reassuring invective, 'Lordy, now you've done it."

They passed at the point where the dunes showed flaky rock-ends and the white rubble began at the upsurge of the mountain. Miguel was tight-lipped with furtive hatred, Toad stared at him blandly with a horrid face; his lip still curled and frozen in distortion. He had always greeted the boy, a little awkward in his loud joviality, but persisting in spite of the rebuff; wanting to make friends because he felt himself that Miguel's supposed jealousy was justified. He saw him now without seeing him, passing like a shadow of Millie that had vaguely come to hurt him.

Miguel lost a step when he had passed; half turned and went hurriedly on, clutching the book. Why hadn't Karl stopped? Why hadn't he called to him with that too-wide grin of his too-small mouth, the loud slang familiarity as if Miguel couldn't hear or couldn't understand? Why all that staring horror and contempt?

Miguel had never had anything against him impersonally. In a strange way he even liked Karl well enough, and was impressed with his handsomeness and size, though these made him conscious of his own spare, square childishness. Also he had dreaded seeing too much of Miss Delaney just now, and it was something of a relief to be able to go twice a week with the smaller, more frequent summer deliveries and leave quickly, with a plausible excuse for his haughtiness. But his superstition was too quick; there was also in Karl's power and beauty and monopolization of Miss Delaney the suggestion of retribution, and it was this that his mind would come back to, and would come back to, and made him steel himself with hatred against the mocking openness of all that blonde bright cheer. No doubt, he thought, Karl and Miss Delaney were amused by his jealousy, as if he had ever wanted anything from her but her library and her professional advice; well, let them be. But he cared. He had thought to begin learning seriously now that school was out; he was at the grocery every day only till noon, and there was little to do at home but find games for his sister that would leave him stretches of time to himself. But the heaviness of the book he had obstinately chosen depressed him in the close hot room. He was out of patience with St. Augustine and his petty penance: all that squandered emotion over a stolen pear! All that distorted pride at having deserted the poor slut! His own book was worse; he read it over from end to end, for reassurance, and with a sickness of fatigue he realized that all of his best things were imitations; even when he had not realized it he had been stealing. His mind came back to Miss Delaney and her lover, perhaps laughing at him now; worse, perhaps sharing the knowledge of his plagiarism. And down it as he might, ignore it as he could, this image kept coming back to him, over the page, beyond the grocery box, through his sleep, that Miss Delaney, who had never shared anything she respected with anyone but him, was sharing disrespect of him with the sudden stupid foreigner. It became too much for him; he must go to her again, return a book and ask for another, talk about Dickens and Saint Augustine; carefully, not daring her to confront him with his crime—he would be lost if she did—but offering discreetly to make it up, watching her to see how much she knew, and why she was so distant from him.

Now, steel-silent and contemptuous, Karl had passed almost before Miguel could register his look. He waited for the greeting, and faltered, as

it struck him suddenly that he knew; he did
know!

Miguel felt himself burning, augmenting the
fierce slanting heat. His heart was at the nape
of his neck, pounding at the roots of his hair,
beating the rhythm of the lullaby.

> *Eres Paloma blanca*
> *Como la nueve*
>
> *You are, white dove*
> *Like the snow.*
>
> *White dove, snow dove.*

He remembered with unnatural clarity all the
transformations of his theft, wishing to forget
them. It was as it had been before, in his
daydreams, when he had been moving perhaps
in some dark exotic setting, passionately
reciting lines in a foreign tongue to a beautiful
black-eyed princess. Suddenly her face would
become disfigured, and try as he might to
backtrack and recover his daydream, the
woman would become disfigured again, showing
black teeth or three eyes or a jawless bald and
terrible blank. It was the same now with his

own disfiguration of the song he had loved as a child; since the tune would not leave his mind he tried to match the original words to it, but they faded and slid away, and were replaced one by one, with unnatural clarity, by all the successive attempts of his translation.

He remembered as if in the present the night that his deception had first occurred to him. He was stretched out on his stomach on his mother's cot, his elbows balanced at the foot and his head hung above his notebook on the floor. It was a comfortable night for May, even a little breeze through the adobe arch, so his mother padded about more energetically than usual, humming, dusting the plastic crucifix and the ceramic wreath that adorned her altar. He remembered the way his sister whined, wordlessly, and tickled his feet with a chicken feather for attention, and would not let up, so failing to ignore her lie lashed out, "*Vaya! Quiete la boca, Stupida!*" and drew an absent "*Miguelito*", of reproach from his mother. His mother went back to her futile dusting and her humming, raising more dust from the floor than she took from the crucifix. Miguel went back to his notebook. He even remembered the page he was scrawling from the inconvenient position.

You have not touched me yet at all
Dipping your pen in death.
None of the tragedies I recall
Have made me catch my breath.

Having recently made debut
From pencil box and roller skate,
From blocks and Winnie the honoured
Pooh. . .

He was intensely bored. It was pompous, insincere. He had never had a pair of roller skates nor honoured Winnie the Pooh, let alone caught his breath. And for all the romanticism of it, it sloughed into exactly what Miss Delaney did not want; petty images, denial of feeling. All it had to its credit was a forced rhyme and a singsong rhythm. He was angry at Miss Delaney.

He remembered the way he had been roughing the paper with hard black lines, bending the nib of his pen. His mother broke into the words of her tune, pressing the nail of the crucifix more securely into the adobe. She had a heavy, complaining voice, the voice of a fat woman. Idly Miguel translated the words literally as she sang.

You are, white dove,
like the snow,
perched in the river;
and you drink.

For God's sake, white dove,
Come with me. I will help you.

I have a broken wing
The colour of the lily,
I have travelled far on the wind
And I am tired.

He was listening hard suddenly. He tried to
write down the words; in English, as she sang
but even her slow heavy voice went faster than
his hand and lie fell behind her.

I am alone, alone
I am alone, alone
I am alone without a master,
Most alone; without loves
And in a strange village.

He stopped there and let her sing on without
him. He looked over what he had written. "You
are, white dove, like the snow, perched in the

river, and you drink." It was not as forceful as it had seemed to him as a child. More like "lighted on the river bank to drink". But not that; there was more the pain of the broken wing in it: "Fallen to the river brink, fallen to the bank to drink." Something like that.

> *You are, white dove, like the snow*
> *Fallen to the river brink,*
> *Fallen to the bank to drink.*

Brink, bank, drink; it had pleasant tinkling about it, which he wholly accredited to the nursery rhyme. Perhaps the third person? "The white dove is like the snow." No, prosaic. "You are like the snow, dove." Snow dove! "White dove, snow dove." He was excited. He turned a fresh page and rewrote his verse, changing it slightly as he went along.

> *White dove, snow dove*
> *Fallen to the river brink*
> *Drifted to the bank to drink*
> *Snow dove, come with me.*

He worked on it for four days; thinking of almost nothing else, and for two weeks he carried it folded into quarters in his hip pocket, pulling it out now and again to see if it had wilted; changing a comma, trading one word for another with a closer meaning or a lighter lilt or a longer vowel sound. He was always conscious of the fact that he was not really doing anything; it was not his poem, and his game with it was far too unmixed a joy, far too effortless an effort to come under the name of writing. But he was excited and happy. The longer he looked at it, the surer he became that it was good, whether it was stolen or not. And the closer it seemed to him the very blueprint of the poem for which Miss Delaney unmercifully pressed him. He wanted desperately to please her. He felt that, once she had given him her approval, he would be able to do himself what had been done for him. And even as he was ashamed of himself, he was proud of the poem.

The two senses existed in him side by side, on the one hand the indecency of his plagiarism and his worthless game, on the other the astounding, intense personal discovery of the poverty of literal translation:

I have a broken wing
The colour of the lily;

I have travelled far on the wind
And I am tired.

He lay on the ground in the shade of a white cliff one afternoon and dreamed himself into a dove. He cramped his arm awkwardly behind his shoulder until it hurt as if it were broken, and for a long time he lay convinced that he could not lift it. He let the warm wind whistle and moan over him, wafting him into unutterable fatigue.

I have come far; come far,
Come far on a wounded winging;
Travelled the lily-coloured wing
On a wind worn sad of singing.

He had a way of becoming physically involved in the mental work. Each time he sat down to it, after he had passed the stage in which he was doggedly working for Miss Delaney, which was always pervaded with a sense of guilt; after he had begun to work for the words themselves, his whole body rose to the search. He would cup his hand, palm up, and claw at the air, reaching for the meaning, or more gently pulse his fingers in a beckoning. No one ever saw him at it, but occasionally he would see himself, and break his mood by laughing, proud of his own intensity. He was flushed when he wrote. He became conscious of it, and one night took his mother's precious thermometer from its drawer in the altar table. He had a degree and a half. He was greatly impressed, and then suddenly, out of the mood, ashamed, and did not know if it was his effort or his guilt which caused the fever. He did not take his temperature again. But again he became involved in the poem, and again forgot.

> *Stop, white dove;*
> *You are making me cry.*
> *I will give you*
> *The wings to fly.*

The very humour of his literal translation made him wistful, since he wanted to be wistful. The sight of the crooked wing, dragging a path in the river mud, broke his heart. Lilies grew nearby, out of bullrush stalks, dove white, snow white, their flowers like curled and hovering wings. The dove, dragging a weight of gathering mud, faltered and could not reach the feathery shade. He could feel the weight of the sucking mud on the shattered bones. He woke his mother with a sharp intake of breath, and drew from her a drowsy, inarticulate concern.

"Nothing, *mamacita*. I was having a dream."

He bent to the book and wrote in round slow letters, the pen dragging like so much mud on the end of his injured arm.

> *Snow dove, come to me*
> *Weeping at the river brink;*
> *Lily, river, love and I*
> *Weeping at the river brink*
> *For your wounded wind and singing;*
> *We will find you wings to fly.*

He remembered, wishing to forget, Miss Delaney's face on graduation afternoon, below him on a bright blurred background. She smiled wonderfully, her lips slightly parted with pride and awe. He had wanted suddenly to leap down and rush at her, to confess and see her hurt and have it over, to lay the blame on her and make her admit that it was her fault, to be forgiven or not forgiven, anything but that lighted face, basking in his lie. He was not by nature particularly honest; he might have stolen money and rationalized it well enough, even denied his theft in a convincing way. But he suddenly realized the worse than futile theft of Miss Delaney's confidence, and as with the brief ideas he had scribbled in the margins of her books, her very approval seemed somehow the proof of his deception.

He had been following the path out of habit, his eyes on his shoes, the dust and grass passing by in a blur, and when his toe struck the Angleberger back step he woke from his painful reverie with a slight nausea, like seasickness. A lawn chair leaned crookedly against the open door, and from inside came a throaty gurgling sound. Sunblind he stared into the dimmer kitchen, the dim outline of two pairs of buttocks on kneeling figures, like puppets stored in suspension. The one was a padded paunch of red striped pyjama bottoms, the other like unsanded wood draped in lavender crêpe. The weird dim marionettes leaned over a bucket and scouring pads, the woman's wooden hand on the man's rag-stuffed thigh, the man's face swung into the woman's neck, from whence came the erratic liquid sound, like faulty plumbing heard through a wall. As Miguel stared the figures whirled toward him in one motion, their heads together, their buttocks swinging outward as if on strings. Mrs. Angleberger's gurgle erupted in a choking sound and she sprang up woodenly in the feathered shawl, leaving Duncan on the floor, one shoe off, one shoe on, glaring in startled anger.

"You boy!" She spat. "What do you mean? What do you want?" Miguel stared trying to remember his message. Mrs. Angleberger's stiff coiled hair shook weirdly on her head. She was drawn up in rigid dignity, showing the farthest of her extraordinary teeth; she was white and hard, her skin like bone. "Peep Tom!" She screamed at him. "Sneak!" Her eyes burned accusingly, locking his jaw. Did she know too? Did even she know?

"I . . . my mother," he stammered at last. "My....mother can't today."

Mrs. Angleberger reached out with a vicious motion, Miguel stepped instinctively back, but she only snatched at the doorknob with wooden fingers and slammed it to, knocking the lawn chair forward on the grass. Miguel turned and ran, back toward the mountain, back toward the Delaney house, stumbling in the road ruts and on the litter of the vacant lots. He headed straight for the chintz-hung door, through the bonfire debris and the broken glass, cutting a straight path through the winding palm trees and leaping down to the flagstone patio, where he once more stopped short and stared with wan, blanched disbelief. Miss Delaney's shutters were closed, wedged tight together with the warping of long disuse. The windows were flanked with perfect rectangles of deeper mustard, like wallpaper faded around a photograph. It gave the house a look of age and frailty.

Miguel reached for the knob, which turned and clicked with a hollow sound, but did not open. As he did so he caught sight of a scrap of yellow paper protruding beneath the door. It was written in a shaky hand, and his hands shook as he read it.

Miguel,

Will you leave the groceries on the step? I am all right, but I would like to be left alone for a while. I'll leave a note here when I need anything. I think I can trust you not to mention it to anyone?

MISS DELANEY

Miguel thought he would be sick. He wheeled on the porch and sat with his head between his knees, slowly crumpling the paper in his fist.

For a while he thought of nothing but his nausea, then the pounding in his stomach seemed to slow somewhat, and the harsh irony of the sentence, "I think I can trust you not to mention it to anyone?" resounded through his mind. Somewhere deep in him a bitterness began, a muffled sense that the punishment was extreme and out of tone. But he pushed it down to let guilt and discovery swell over him like a sort of cleansing, and began to cry.

When he had finished he smoothed the note and folded it in his pocket, and without looking back at the averted eyes of Millie Delaney's house, he began the slow walk back to the Emporium, where Gallencamp would be awaiting him with another hostile face.

$$XX$$

The last shutter latched against the sun, Millie Delaney watched her world's reflection above the mantelpiece. "Now," she said aloud, "now I have no window but a mirror." And in that summer of her seclusion, slowly a dust settled on the tapestry sofa, on her shoulders, on her soul.

It might have been no more than that time when every woman realizes her own imperfectibility, and the imperfectibility of circumstance; when the death of hope that is maturity takes her, and she harbours the lack that she has always known, takes it to herself, calls it by name, and no longer expects that it will someday leave her. But in Millie Delaney it was more than loneliness. The people of Sintiempo noticed the streets' drab absence of Millie Delaney, listened for her small bird's voice and watched, without quite realizing it, for the feather-black of her hair and the shimmering soft dresses. In the grocery store the women spoke of it, Mrs. Wesch and Mrs. Angleberger and Avril Hilton, with some taint of genuine regret, and a greed that would have been less veiled for anyone else's scandal.

"Millie's closed up the place."

"Oh lordy, Toad Ormerod's gone for sure. I tell you, the girls are a fool one after the other these days."

"Oh, he's gone no doubt. Millie's good for getting left alone."

"This is different, Avril Hilton. Jilting is worse than somebody's dying, you mark me."

"She's a broken heart, that's what she is."

"That Toad, Toad Ormerod."

But in Millie Delaney it was more than heartbreak. Something that had bubbled like a sudden stream, miraculous from the bedrock of her life, not dammed but dwindling, had gone at last altogether dry. It was not that Toad Ormerod had left her, but it was partly that he had come at all; not that he had stolen her heart, as the women of Sintiempo believed, but that he had left her only the gift of a soul-deep satiation. So that she had been able to say, "Yes, this is real love. Yes, I know now; this is what love really is." And being able to say it, had had to say it, to herself as well as Toad; "Well, now I know the mysteries of bed; yes, now I do know all of that."

She remembered that once she had begged her mother for a toy sewing machine for so many months that the begging had become a chant instead of desire. And when it was finally given her, she had carried it around all day, not playing with it, but repeating to herself with feigned delight, "I have a sewing-machine, I really do have a sewing-machine," and had known a vague regret for the loss of wanting. Now, pleased with boasting to herself of her new knowledge, she knew the depth of the loss of mystery, and at the time when life, which had never pampered her, suddenly offered her everything, she backed away, "Is that *all*?" The seclusion had begun in her even then, before the shutters closed, and Toad Ormerod had gone; sullen, angry, confused, loud, in love with her.

XXI

In a small community, a "homogenized" community, as Milton Delaney's slipping tongue had once pronounced at a Rotary Club banquet, impressing no one but himself with the accuracy of his mistake; in a homogenized community, there is likely to be an acceptance of the familiar weird with what seems to be a metropolitan nonchalance. In a town where an unknown cocker spaniel is an object of curiosity and even of grave concern, the village idiot is apt to be taken for gentle granted.

And thus, like a mother with a cretin child, after the initial confusion and disbelief, Sintiempo accepted the closing of the Delaney house and the interment of the loved but always slightly unorthodox girl. Mrs. Angleberger, if the truth were known, and she was the last to know it, was not wholeheartedly anxious to have the spectacle arrested. Having been Millie's only regular acquaintance, she was looked to now as rather an authority on the girl's unhappy motives. Her protective tone returned. Millie, it appeared, had been practically a daughter to her, and hers was the

hopeless heartache now of a mother for her
jilted girl. The universal aura of romance
transformed itself into a rather more
satisfactory indignation and pity. Toad was
generously libelled as a fool, a jilt, a city slicker
and a ruffian.

And indeed he seemed to warrant it. He was
not graceful at despair. He drank, and abused
his fellow workers who, not understanding the
change, only renewed their good natured
derision until he silenced them one by one with
a broken nose or a festering eye. The role did not
suit his temperament, and even drunk he raged
with an unconvincing violence. He swore,
smashed glasses, gambled himself into debt
with the bogus bravado of a grade B cowboy
star. The ladies made noises with their tongues
on the roofs of their mouths, and pitying Millie
Delaney averred her well rid of him.

Not that they were overly inclined to interfere.
Avril telephoned once with an offer of peanut
butter cookies, but finding the telephone off the
hook, gave the batch to a charity bazaar, and
offered instead a short prayer for Millie's broken
heart. "Millie knows how to take care of herself,"
Lena said in the face of the facts. Nonetheless,
she too made one attempt, with Duncan

doggedly and disapprovingly at her heels. She circled the mustard stucco twice, remarking with a melancholy co-operation of throat and teeth the crisp brown death of the pyracantha bushes, yodelling loudly at the shutters. And they returned home. Lena thought, but not seriously, of speaking to Karl. She had no intention of talking sense into the head of a man who no longer even bathed.

The grocery boy fell briefly ill, which was rather a nuisance with the mid-week deliveries, especially as the illness of his mother left extra housework to do in half a dozen homes. An unreliable pair. But on the third morning after his absence Miguel appeared again, no less sullen than ever, with an order pencilled in Millie's hand, and the deliveries resumed. He was not altogether well, though, Mrs. Gallencamp confided to a select group counting ration tickets into her unregarded palm. He cried rather a lot, and was apt to fly into a rage if he heard them speaking of Millie Delaney. A schoolboy crush no doubt, rather sweet, but there was something odd about him. She doubted he'd be much good, when the time came, in the quarry.

XXII

She settled into the rocker with a weightless purposelessness like settling dust, into the humid subterranean darkness, heat without light, into the leather cup of seventeen years' human weight, buried now, decaying now, diffusing now a subterranean humid heat to the starved roots of imported maple trees. Or not yet perhaps. For how many years does a steel casket keep out the rain? Rough iron arrow heads found in the Lenajidak hills almost perfectly intact, almost a thousand years after they cleaved the life of their victims. A thousand years perhaps? Two thousand years for the strength of modern steel, with the eyes ignobly closed and the limp lips withered into the chasm of toothless gums? From what obscure strained grasping after immortality does the phenomenon of the weather-proof casket derive? She laughed a little and began to rock.

"I am alone, alone. . ." Consider Lucretius. Consider the gifted fool. As certain that the world was composed of atoms as he was that the mind was lodged in the breast. Human certainty has never had much to do with truth, and human uncertainty only slightly more. Yet Lucretius must be right. That woman only began to decay, not yet feeding the roots of any physical thing, with not enough soul to speak of at any time. Into what force of being had passed one minor obsession for the harmonica, one weakness for the domestic epigram? Did she admonish Gabriel to wear his rubbers and lead the harps in "Old Black Joe"? No not immortality, but as some single cell of her hidden eyes would furnish the matrix of a cactus spine, so now on some plane of existence for which we have no diagram, the decomposing elements of a late Victorian mind regrouped themselves toward a modern embryo. Lucretius must be right. Soda and vinegar mixed in a glass rage and rise, strain spluttering toward a height and babble down, an oblique of slime. There is your soul. There's your soul for you, the chemical reaction of physical elements in a kitchen glass. And for that, for the almighty preservation of soda and vinegar you make your strong steel caskets and your symphonies and your poems. Lucretius must be right.

She rocked a whining symphony in the straining wood, viewing with dissatisfaction the smooth strength of her slender hands where they lay along the arms, the oblong patch of tender red from her fingers to her wrist where the boiling fat had fallen. The hands should be old. They should be wrinkled and callous, powerless and gnarled. She hid the tender scar in her lap and rocked into nonexistence the memory of that morning and that quarrel; rocked measuring time, which does not exist, rocked so many simultaneous whining notes in the point of eternity.

And is art a better alloy than iron and carbon? The immortality of Lucretius? The immortality of Shakespeare? The immortality of Plato? Sixty thousand years perhaps before the language dies away. Six hundred thousand years before the human being no longer is, and is replaced by another reptile of a different brand of vinegar. And is sixty thousand years any longer than sixty? If it takes two weeks to love and conceive a child and cease to love, can it take so long to conceive a universe and let another die away?

"I am alone, alone...."

I am a human metronome, I mark and measure time, she thought, and then: Oh, God how far the mind will go to keep the mind from what it fears to know . . I am alone, alone . . . I am a human metronome, I am a glass of vinegar, I am . . . going to have a baby.

Though she was not hungry, she went to the kitchen and ate a tomato. She sliced it into quarters with a once fat butcher knife worn to the shape of a huge door key with a quarter-century of carving. Stainless steel. She ate leaning over the sink so that the juice dripped in round red and golden globules toward the drain, staring at the weathered closure of the shutters, where the sun, without advancing to the room, outlined the crooked cracks.

Not guilt, not rebellion, no more of raging against the circumstance than gratitude for realizing at last the hollowness at the world's core, but as if the physical existence of an infinitesimal amoeba created its counterpart in the mind, so that whatever she turned to, the fact existed, and she would come to it again: some electric wave of association—the word tree on its way to the idea of tall in her brain—would ripple over the cell of the fact, and it would be there again: she was going to have a baby. She argued with the fact, she wheedled, she aborted it. She was not sure. The shock of the loss of virginity is great enough to wrench the system wildly from its cycle, she said, like a moon thrown out of its orbit by a falling meteor. But as she said it, said it aloud, for she spoke often to herself to break the dank silence built on the stale vibrations of harmonica music; as she said it, she could hear the laughter of the two infinitesimal cells in league against her. For she could not think of herself as shocked. Drained, dried, dead perhaps, but not shocked. She stooped one morning to retrieve from the carpet the book she had flung there the night before, so that it lay with its covers splayed and its pages sagging into each other with their own weight. She stayed stooping over it for a moment, not reading it but without the energy to rise, and when she stood at last a wave of dizziness washed over her, setting into motion the persistent mocking cell, and she dropped the book again. There was a word for it, she told herself. Perchysis, peripsychosis, psychocenisis, something: the fear of having a child can create the symptoms of pregnancy. But she could not remember the word, and she was not afraid.

She was not in the least afraid. Her very weakness began to seem the potential of a great dull enduring strength. At first she would not have the baby, she would not have it. But then she conceived out of emptiness, out of boredom, that she could have it. That she could give birth to it herself, in the closet she had made of the house, like a domestic animal. She could bring it not into the world, but into a sun of her own making, so that it would believe the universe bounded by the bookcase and the weathered warping of the kitchen shutters. It had never occurred to her to hide the disgrace of her child from Sintiempo, but it occurred to her now to hide the disgrace of Sintiempo from her child. A child who would believe in no existence but the inside of the house, would expect no escape but the beauty of the books, would have no pattern of a mind but the mind of Millie Delaney and of Plato and of Shakespeare. Never to see the promise flicker and die in another human being. And at the thought of Toad the amoeba in her body and the amoeba in her brain writhed and smiled.

Another girl might have felt the relief of his being gone, and have pouted a little and begun again with a look of weary wisdom. Another girl might have shuddered at her stupidity and imagined a man with darker hair and a firmer voice. Another girl might have remembered her reckless freedom at the death of the aged drone, and from having ignored it, made a half-truth into a whole explanation. But Millie had hoped too vaguely and too profoundly ever to have been disappointed by the failure of minor hopes. Karl had been everything that her life was not; and becoming everything that her life had been, no new daydream came to override the disgust and the disappointment.

Except one daydream. Of a human mind that could not disappoint her because, wilfully, she could create it, as now against her will she created a body. She stood on the stairway, her eyes intense and black, her mouth in a tight crooked line, grasping down the banister at a tiny hand, staring as if into infinite space toward the book-filled wall of the dark room. "Do you know?" she said aloud, "that from here you can see Athens and Chaos and Chelsea?" And with the listless intensity of revenge, she began to want the child.

XXIII

July hit hot and dry like all Julys. The last boll burst from the cottonwood trees, and the thistly fruit powdered into the dust, the caterpillars appeared and wove cocoons of the debris. Gourmets, they stripped the rich green meticulously from the leaves and left the naked veins, and when they had fed hung themselves in communal sacks of transparent web, fist sized and heavy, from the razed branches. Little girls in Sintiempo, who sometimes squatted alone to watch fat grey and orange worms writhe over the pebbles in their path, and sometimes poked a twig into a jet velvet polka dot, ran screaming from the same bug held at the end of a schoolboy's arm, and cried, and were genuinely afraid. The boys threw stones at the cocoons, pooling their marbles, which were coloured glass and manufactured in Cincinnati, for the first to cleave the bag from the branch. No one could, so they reached for them with baseball bats, and succeeded finally with a hoe. When the bag thudded with a liquid crunch into the dust and the caterpillars fled from it in radii of slow rippling, leaving a mound of white larvae like a burst balloon, they felt rather uneasy and parted toward home. The next day they climbed a tree and poured kerosene on a larger cocoon, and set it on fire. Though they had done the same the year before, it seemed rather new for a week or two; then they tired of it and went back to mumbledy peg, and the remaining caterpillars, which were sufficiently numerous, dozed toward their September wings.

The cacti lived stoically, to the annual admiration of the townsfolk, but it was too dry for even their blooms, and nothing but zinnias were worth the planting. Zinnias were planted, and stood in rigid, unflowerlike rows in shallow trenches lining the walks.

In mid-July the Anglebergers went to Railton for a conference of county principals and superintendents. There was, rather to the surprise of Duncan, who had not considered that it infringed upon his professional concerns, a good deal of talk about the war. Someone quoted Winston Churchill's recent remark that "the end of the beginning" had been reached, and impressively employing the phrase as a warning toward continued vigilance, conjured the educators to combat evil foreign influence in the impressionable young. Toad Ormerod was the only foreign influence that Duncan could recall, and he whispered sadly to Lena that it would be a better idea to educate the educators, there. Lena nodded confirmation, but shushed him even as she nodded.

There were a particular number of resolutions passed concerning the rise in the birth-rate, and the overcrowded schoolroom conditions to be expected a decade hence. Remembering the number of early pregnancies in Sintiempo now, Duncan was profoundly moved by the inexplicably penetrating influence of war, and he adopted a premature concern over the impending educational disaster. Even after they had returned to Sintiempo and their voyage had been duly recorded in the *Sintiempo Sun*, he continued to talk about it, citing articles and quoting statistics from the two state papers he had bought in Railton. The predictable shortage of schoolteachers was inextricably connected in his mind with the fact that, if Millie did not come out soon, he should have to look for a substitute for fall. Not wishing to mention this directly, for fear that his wife would advise a course of action, he fairly thundered the necessity for foresighted organization. Lena let him thunder, sympathizing from the depths of her throat as she ran the carpet sweeper over the throw rugs and tidied his dog-eared newspapers under her stack of *Readers' Digests*.

He was engaged in such a lecture one morning when the groceries arrived, and after a moment's pause at the knock and the opening of the door, he continued. Since the morning of their discovery in the compromising throes of marital affection, it had been Duncan and Lena's policy to ignore the grocery boy altogether.

"War babies, not a problem you can solve just by solving," he was saying. "Nope. Reverberations. Re-ver-ber-ations. You don't get enough extra teachers and schools, you're going to have a generation of illiterates. You think illiterates are interested in being school-teachers? Nope. They'll bring you up another one like them. Saying you do, you manage it somehow and get the kids through okay, what'll happen then? After they're out. Into the world. Going to have a surplus left over in the profession, unemployment, a lot of empty schoolhouses drawing taxes for upkeep and not worth a furthing, not worth a fur-thing. Make the teaching profession very unpopular, that. Next generation nobody'll want to be teachers,

225

you'll have a shortage and it'll start all over again. "Reverberations," he reverberated as the screen door slammed. He was wondering whether, at a pinch, he might teach the seventh and eighth grades himself, and hope that Millie would get over Toad by Christmas.

That afternoon Miguel sat in the sun and opened his notebook on a blindingly blank page.

"7/18/43", he inscribed, and chewed at the cap of his once sleek pen, which was scarred with tooth marks almost to its point.

"But in that war there was no birth rise. The usual numbers were eliminated, but none were manufactured to take their place. Journalists dutifully recorded the unhistoric, unpatriotic fact, but the foxholed sons of journalists lay snuggling with their bayonets, cheek to blade, and would not procreate."

He wrote invariably now of things he did not know. He clung tenaciously to words he had read and never heard pronounced. Jungles and battlefields and aged orientals crossed his pages like an exotic picture book, and they were as likely as not to be procrusted, or oligopolous, or hoarding velleities. The notebook was his escape and his condemnation. He was never happy with what he wrote, he knew that every note rang false, but the falseness fitted his idea of himself, and he would not suffer a familiar shape; no bird, no lily, no tear and nothing Mexican, to recall his ugly failure. The opening of the book invariably recalled it, but if he steeled himself through those moments he might, he might, he might and sometimes did, forget his guilt in something musical and unfamiliar of his own making. There was no point in an effort to drown himself in his physical work. The work was not hard enough, it was a routine designed for idle thinking, and there was at any moment the danger that he would hear some word of Millie Delaney's broken heart. When those moments came he wanted to silence the voices with some indefinite burst of violence. He knew well enough of Millie Delaney's broken heart, and only he knew who had broken it. Only he, and perhaps the man who was also being punished for his sin.

But the man who was being punished for his sin knew nothing at all: did not know why he had once thought war the only insane affront to human reason, did not know why he had chosen Sintiempo for his escape, did not know why he had fallen in love with the sort of woman he did not like. He did not know why he drank, for his unhappiness changed in kind but not in degree when he was drunk, and drunk his desire for Millie Delaney became a cruel rage for which there was no name but lust.

Unlike Millie, he had fallen in love many times, and had known the failure of the moment when falling in love must change its nature to being in love, or cease to be. He had known many times the boredom of that failure, with all its accompanying self-reproach and resolution, its irritations and maudlin scenes. But he could not transfer his knowledge to any symptom in Millie Delaney's masque of love. He showed his anger when he was angry, his boredom when he was bored, his loving when he loved. He could not see past even Millie's waning smile. He did not know why she had suddenly no longer loved him. He only knew with a searing certainty that he was despised by the only thing it had ever been worth his trouble to care about, and that through hate, Millie Delaney had become, quite literally, insane.

The three certainties settled with the finality of all self-evident fact—that Millie had closed the house because she had been jilted; that Millie had closed the house because a fool of a boy in whom she believed had treacherously deceived her; that Millie had closed the house because she was insane. The first of these, supported by its number, lost its intensity of interest in time, except perhaps to Duncan Angleberger, whom it professionally disturbed. The others gained the momentum of martyrdom, like all truths held in the face of accepted falsehood.

Truth held in the face of accepted falsehood. She was going to have a baby. She did not speculate about their speculations, but the rest of it, July, transgressed her sanctuary. An occasional caterpillar wormed over the weather stripping of the kitchen door, and unable or unanxious to retrace its crawl, spun its cocoon on the baseboard and went to sleep. July was in her mind then with unwanted vividness; the stripped leaves and their tremulous branchings of golden vein; the golden gashes in the bark where a misthrown stone had brought the summer sap thickly to the surface; the rigid zinnias whose garish colours no painter, out of artistic discretion, would ever care to catch. Duncan would be in Railton invoking progress in the form of a spelling book with bigger type. The talk, even among old friends who did not have to clutch for conversation, would be of the weather, and shot through with prideful dread of the impending August. They would be hanging their thermometers on the shady sides of metal clothes-poles to catch the highest allowable reading, and boasting in horror that it was one seventeen in the shade. In the shade the cows would chew and crank their tails, standing and lying scattered in dull independence of each other and their masters, indifferently blinking fly-matted lids. While corralled by the adjoining fence, gelded into unity, the steer would paw the heat and lumber in a mass, turning together from the outer edge, in a rippling pressure of hide on hide, as dominoes fall.

As she had seen it many times before, against a quartzite cliff undulating in the heat, under a dusty tamarisk in obese and candid grace a couple of ranch wives would stop to chat, gesturing languidly in the shimmering air, rocking a market basket on an arm.

These were the things she was denied. Because, go closer, within distance of listening, and all the grace will fall away. Perhaps, ". . . flushed a diaper down the drain. It ain't the first time he's done it. I gave him a hiding, believe you me, but that'll do nothing for the linoleum where it's warped, and the price of plumbing . .." or, "one of them A-1 beer ads with the fellow sleepin' on his saddle and dreaming up a naked girl in the clouds—you know the one? I told him I wasn't goin' to have it in my living room, framed like The Last Supper, he could hang it in the loft if he had a mind to . . ." or even, in earlier years, ". . . a pretty head of hair on his Mrs., but don't she know it though, she and her fancified Eastern ways. . . ." Memory like a weather-proof casket preserving a horizon's worth of ugliness as a graceful lie. Her mind did not know what it meant, but beauty is falsehood, truth ugliness perhaps would do, and sick with July she went to bed in the middle of the afternoon.

She moved always in a haze of unreality, less like a dream than like a perpetual drunkenness, because nothing she touched seemed any more real than the hand that touched it. She kept a conscientious record of the date, beneath a calendar motif this year, of a cowboy riding into the lurid sunset; crossing off each day as she perceived it dead through shutter cracks and doorsills, motivated by a sort of negative satisfaction that was her only source of energy.

The length of a lifetime alone in the accumulating dank of the darkened house had never occurred to her, nor did it occur to her now, but the length of nine months waiting until April and the child seemed unfairly long. What is to be done with time?

July 12th. Behind the calendar, between the shelves, over the rough-cut pages of dusty books the paper wall of grey on grey defining time. A dark raised line described a curve and doubled back upon itself; wriggled no wider than a hair in meaningless arcs, broke and began again, tied a knot in its tail and cut across the path of its own wanderings, retraced its pattern upside down. And from a foot away no more than a pebbly mottling, from the stairway only an endless block of grey. Grey time, time wandering, memory paper stamped in paper time. She understood.

July 15th. The ides of July. Funny the way she never could divest her mind of the sense of every mid-month as an ides. The ides of July are come; aye, Caesar but not gone. What's to be done with July15th? A dark grey line described a curve and doubled back upon itself, wriggled no wider than a hair in meaningless arcs—½ lb. pot., 1 lb. gr. round, head let.—and pencilling her scant needs for Miguel she unwillingly recalled his own round hand. Not that she missed him, not that she cared what he was doing, he the most futile of that futile group. But the way the first letters of a page stood thick and straight, and began to slant, and then deteriorated into an old illegibility where he became excited with his words. The way an oblique stroked double line would point to the preferred and more precise choice over a heavily crosshatched adjective. He would be recording the cocooning of the caterpillars now, in harsh and caustic images. Not that it mattered. Nor was she thinking of Toad at all, except to think that she was not thinking of him.

July 18th. She went idly through drawers and musty trunks; recreating her childhood in an effort to obliterate it and destroy its mementos, actually preserving for future need almost everything she had intended to destroy. An oilcloth bib still stained with the juice of strained spinach and apricots, the taffeta dress of the day of growing palms, a rag-stuffed doll with black glass pupils which goggled in celluloid eyes. Googoo Eyes, she had called it. Poor Googoo Eyes interred alive on a closet shelf, because she never could quite bear to send it at Christmas time with the other outgrown toys to the charity basket. Poor Googoo Eyes unsleeping rocked against her still flat belly in folded arms. Would a child not wonder where a doll came from, or why there were not others, or why books spoke of them, or of trees? Would a child believe as she was told (it would be she, of course) that everything outside the boundary walls was a game, a product of the mind? Seeing that some doorknobs turned, would she not wonder why others stuck? Or why in books the children ran in grass, and died, and went to school? But rocking Googoo Eyes unsleeping in the painful artificial light of the storage closet, the thoughts passed through her mind like artificial obstacles to a preaccomplished fact, like the preposterous objections of the insane to plain reality. She was taken, in another tone of mind, like a voice reciting poetry suddenly dropping into prose, with the wry idea of making baby clothes, but after an evening of cutting up white organdy curtains, she let the filmy scraps lie on a bedroom chair, without even the impetus of cynicism to proceed.

The twenty first. Sore throat and running nose; unaccustomed to the stuffiness no doubt. A head cold in July; how inappropriately, in contrast to the imagistic measles, mumps and chicken-pox, a cold is named. Fire in the nostrils, smoke in the eyes, a warm thick liquid in the bones, and even the temporary chill after a flush of fever less a chill than the shudder that keeps vibrating after an electric shock. And how unbearably hot July.

The twenty-second. She stayed in bed till noon, weak enough not to be restless, sleeping a healthy lot. It was not until after toast and tea that it occurred to her how inappropriately she stayed in the master bedroom. Feverish and coughing she returned to the blue rectangle of her childhood, but was dissatisfied with it, the room belonging rightfully to the daughter of the house, and she settled at last under the knit coverlet of Geegee's tiny bed, in Geegee's tiny room where the very walls decayed, and the doors, the springs, the woodwork sung of an old harmonica. My headaches, and a drowsy numbness pains. . . . At what a glowing desert's distance health seems to a body obsessed with its weak achingness. Heaven itself must have been invented by a convalescent. As incapacitated as we are by simple fever, as unable to rest with knees bent or arms folded or back arched . . . think of the normal state of health as a head-cold, and think then what might be done by a body in real health. We have such a fixed and petty idea of the norm. Suppose the uterus in the human female were so placed that it grated against the dorsal epidermis of the stomach at every step, at every turn, at every muscle's move of the middle anatomy, and thereby made a perpetually growing ulcer the norm of every female adult. Suppose the human mind were not so placed that it grated against the uterus at every step of thought, at every memory's move in the upper anatomy, so that realization was not perpetually growing ulcer in the mind of every. . . .

July 24th. Up with nothing to show for her pains but a throatful of phlegm and an order for kleenex on the doorstep. She had been reading again *Great Expectations* in her bed, which lent itself with musty grace to Geegee's room. She had a rich red leatherbound copy of the book, with Victorian penline drawings of Miss Havisham decaying in seclusion and a brocade wedding dress. Catching up with the neglected calendar, Millie caught sight of herself in the mantel mirror, and was dismayed to fury, in spite of the hollow cheeks and hard round eyes, by her youth and her contemporary good looks.

Anger, and a restlessness that seemed to be of her skin itself—What's to be done with time? She dismissed the unsewn organdie scraps, shed one book after another unopened from the shelves, walked about from cupboard to bureau opening and closing drawers. In one of them she came across a baby tooth that she had lost at seven, wrapped in a wad of cotton in a peanut butter jar. She was aware that the keepsake made her desperately nervous, but she would not yield to an image, more nearly motherly than anything she had felt before, of her own child's first pearl-perfect cutting teeth. She wilfully forced herself instead to think of teeth in abstract; of Geegee's dead stub of gum, of the dizzying pattern of acoustical tile on the ceiling of Dr. Kregg's office as one stared at it waiting for the drill. Of the spreading deadness after a needle of novocaine. Yes that was it, her mind retreated to its old habit of instant symbolism, that was the way her whole body and her mind felt now. Existence like a tongue run over a deadened mouth roof, finding it as always there, but awaking no response, the self touching the self; and feeling only half of touch.

Yes that was it. Love as novocaine. At first Karl's elbow brushing her breast had flushed her with exquisite pain, but with familiarity she had died to him piece by piece, until his shoulder was no more than the efficient comfort of the dentist's padded chair, his searching tongue might as well have been a drill in her unfeeling mouth. The lip curled in cruel passion inches above her helpless head, like a dentist's smile of malicious reassurance, "This won't hurt, there's a good girl, this won't hurt!" And lying waiting watching beyond the dizzying pattern of the ceiling rise and fall . . . she shuddered and crumpled her face in her hands, and for the first time since the first breakfast of their brief life together, she cried.

July 26th. Not meaning to, at night she looked outside. The dining-room, which had never been much used since her mother's death, she seldom entered now. But that night she broke a glass and went to replace it from the corner cupboard. She chose a heavy bottomed tumbler and stood up to turn out the light.

The shutters of the dining-room were different from the others, of a more delicate and elegant design, to fit the slender majesty of the French mahogany furniture. Where the others were heavy vertical blocks of wood, these were made of slender slats of polished bamboo, set horizontally in a narrow frame. They looked solid when the light was on, but in the split second of her eyes' adjustment to the dark, they became a skrim, and revealed hazily beyond a slope of moonlit dune, and a fragile crescent hung low above a violet mountain. She snapped the light on and off, on and off, and like a sombre shadow-show the window flashed into solidity, faded into a sky-wide scene of gold and violet. She noted that she would have to board the window more securely before the child came, but of course there was no hurry about that, and somehow it did not get done. Perhaps in order to remind herself, she found ways to pass through the dining-room at night, and with an offhand gesture clicked the light switch back and forth, watching the moon wax on the motionless horizon.

XXIV

’Ria Laureado had a high, round rhythmical voice, even in speech a very singing in the wilderness sort of voice, which she was not overly fond of using. Her habitual muteness had the sullen mark of her older brother’s, and Señora Laureado had been known to pray aloud in the presence of friends for God to send her, whichever appertained, the ability or the will to learn to talk. By her sixth year it was clear that she could, but did not choose to. Señora Laureado neglected, illegally, but without much danger of arrest, to send her to school.

But after Miguel had been perfected in his English accent, learning Millie’s method along with her lesson, he was pleased to pass his knowledge on to his sister. He had enjoyed the transformation from taught to teacher, it did not particularly matter in which language— "Look, ’Ria, watch me, curl your tongue behind your teeth like a garter snake,” or, “Pretend your cheeks are full of a hundred and forty toasted almonds,” or, “Make your mouth round; you’re a coyote howling at the moon.” He was sufficiently imaginative to make it, occasionally, worth her while. He admitted to no very active affection for his little sister, but he would be damned, he told himself, if he would stick to the grocery routine to feed a mute. He feigned a helpless incomprehension when she wanted anything, until she asked for it in a grammatical sentence, or at least a recognizably enunciated word. Occasionally he found the time to show her what she had said on a scrap of paper, and though her pleasure was never so great as his in this game of teaching, she began to recognize begrudgingly a few letters of his home-made primer.

And was he otherwise rewarded for his pains? He was. Now in a round high rhythmical voice, an ingrained plaintive echo of Señora Laureado sorting ill with the careful enunciation of his own efforts, sitting in the dirt and threading the beads of a broken rosary on the prongs of a scrap of chicken wire, over and over she sang the first two lines of her mother's lullaby.

> *"Eres paloma blanca*
> *Como la nieve ..*
> *Eres paloma blanca*
> *Como la nieve...."*

"Stop it, 'Ria," Miguel said.

She stopped it and chewed on a matted lock, drawing an S-shaped breath through hair and teeth, exhaling it in a shushing sound as she sighted through the hole of a bead. A thirty-five watt bulb hung naked above her head and cast her squat shadow over her work, as it made Miguel's bent knees eclipse his page and pen. He shifted his bottom back on the mattress, more firmly against the wall, and held the book on the downward slope of his shins to catch the light.

"7/31/43."

He wrote the numbers three times on top of each other and chewed at his pen. He shifted the cumbersome book back to his thighs and narrowed his eyes in its direction, measuring the indentation of an unbegun paragraph. His stomach growled at its own liquidity, and 'Ria laughed, thereby releasing the lock of hair; which swung stroking her sunsuit shoulder strap with a shiny point, like a paint brush of black oil. Her mouth unoccupied then, she rehearsed again her latest acquisition.

> *"Eres paloma blanca*
> *Como. . ."*

" 'Ria," said Miguel, "if you don't stop singing that, mother will slap your face when she gets home." The song suspended itself on a long drawn note at his voice; and grinning slyly then from the corners of cached black eyes, 'Ria completed:

"*. . .O la nieve.*"

Her mother had never lifted a padded palm against her.

It was after ten o'clock. A thirty-five watt moon was caught on the claws of a Saguaro's upstretched arm, beyond the open door, along the road, in the direction of Señora Laureado's expected return. The cleaning woman's health had unaccountably improved with the onset of the real prostration weather. Not unrelated, fat Mrs. Wesch was rude enough to say in her much blunter way than this, to the fact that her (Mrs. Wesch's) house was damp air cooled, while hers (Señora Laureado's) wasn't. However that may be, in the cleaning woman's absences, dust had collected on the damp air cooled collecting bottles in Mrs. Wesch's bathroom cupboard, and Miguel's mother held to her attack past dark, in order to regain the taken ground.

"Eres paloma Blanca
Como la nieve,
Eres paloma blanca
Como la nieve,
Eres paloma blanca. . . ."

"That", said Miguel, "is a rude filthy song which ugly little girls sing when they are marched into reformatory prisons to be beaten by fat black matrons with rubber hoses."

'Ria raised her voice and the corners of her mouth in genuine elation. Miguel bent back to his page and clenched the pen in slightly twitching fingers, awkwardly stopping one ear with his right shoulder and the other with his right middle finger, his elbow cocked straight over his head.

"It was he," Miguel wrote self-consciously and frowning with fierce concentration, "the same Mack Spoon. He'd been muddied about a bit, a little arid behind the ears; changed, jaded, wizened and somewhat wisened, but surely it was he.

"Eres paloma blanca
Como la nieve,
Eres paloma blanca

Como la nieve,
Eres paloma blanca. . . .

"He listed slightly away from the rain and glared with hard dry eyes at the passers-by, cursing them one and all, as I could see, for the personal affront of owning umbrellas. Under a neon awning I slowed, stopped and offered him mine.

"Como la nieve,
Como la nieve,
Como la nieve.

"Eres paloma como,
Blanca la nieve,
Blanca paloma como
Eres la nieve,
Blanca nieve como
Eres la paloma. . . .

"I remembered our last conversation, in that ostentatious San Francisco bar where the bellied barmaid showed her shoulder mole in the mirror as she poured. He had been talking about a clean break, poor Mack, Mack indiscreet, silly Mack, Mack Spoon.

*"Como paloma como
Eres blanca eres,
Como nueres eve
blanco lo polomo. . . ."*

"A clean break like a crayon, I supposed he had in mind, leaving a sharp neat drawing edge and exposing only a little round of waxy granules, coloured evenly across. Whereas Max was brittle like a paloma. . . ." Miguel stared at the word which had taken shape under his pen as if in defiance of the nib's path, and then shoved the notebook on the floor, into 'Ria's box of beads, which rattled and sprawled and rolled in all directions over the uneven and uncovered floor. The notebook cover struck her knee, at which she winced and bit her lips and raised her voice still louder.

*"Eres paloma blanca
Coma la nieve!"*

"Get out of here," Miguel said. 'Ria sprang up and let her handful of beads scatter with the others, coming forward to where he sat and standing over him, an almost comic intensity of stubbornness wrinkling her childish forehead.

246

Miguel slapped her hard on her bare shoulder and with a bare foot on her thigh shoved her toward the door. "Get out, I said. Play outside. I don't want you."

"S'NOCHE!" 'Ria screamed, turning.

"I don't care what time it is," Miguel yelled back. "*Vaya!* I don't want you!"

Deciding that he meant it, delighted with the unprecedented liberty, 'Ria scampered out the door and down the moonward path, particularly pleased that he did not, like her mother, call after her to watch out for snakes.

Miguel retrieved his notebook from the floor and shuffled its pages together. He lay the notebook on the bed and the open pen beside it, put on his shoes, twisted the tap and drank a glass of tepid water in one draught. He took off his shoes, stood brooding at his mother's altar for a moment, put on his shoes, sat down on the bed. He opened the notebook backwards and propped it again in the shadow on his thighs, smoothing it, smoothing it as if to soothe it into obedience. Then he bent forward until his flat

nose almost touched the pen, and began to
write.

July 31st

Dear Miss Delaney,

My little sister has spilled her rosary beads,
and my thoughts are lying like them, scattered,
rolling in all directions in the dust. Believe me
that this letter is harder to write than anything
I have tried to write except one poem, even
harder than that. I have wanted to come to you
and explain, but too much of me depends on you
to risk it all in one wrong moment, and the right
moment has never seemed to come. It was better
to run away, I thought, to make a clean break,
like a crayon breaks, leaving a sharp neat
drawing edge and exposing only a little round of
waxy granules, coloured evenly across. If I have
not done it, it is because I am like a pencil, and
my cleanest break would be a splintering,
jagged and with chipping paint, and leaving a
great grey vein of graphite raggedly exposed.
But now it seems there is no other way.

I do not pretend that what I did I did for you.
I did, but only because I could not myself go on
without your faith. I believed somehow that if I
did what you asked of me once, I would be free
to fit my words together as they came—almost,

248

I'll play your game and afterwards we'll play mine. I swear to you at the time I did not even realize what I was doing. My mother was singing her lullaby, and I took it and translated it, and it almost seemed that I was fulfilling my part of a bargain. I wanted to please you, for my own sake I admit, insist, but I did not want to deceive you. The way to hell is paved. . . .

My sister has learned the lullaby, and everything that I, that we, have wanted to get away from in Sintiempo has come and settled in her voice. Look at it if you can as an ill wind that will carry me away from here. I'll make it up to you. I'll write, and write to you, and though I don't expect you to forget, I hope that someday you will be able to forgive me. Please do not worry, there must be groceries to carry in San Francisco, there must be paper and pencils there. I shall be thinking of you, and working as always for-you-for-myself. Forgive me,

love,
MIGUEL

Grimacing painfully Miguel snapped shut the book and hooked his pen on the cover. He tied the sleeves of a sweater about his waist and stretching on tiptoe lifted down a small clay water jug. Three dollars and fifty cents. He stuffed two of the dollar bills in the hip pocket of his jeans, replaced the jug, and clutched the notebook stomach high.

Outside the moon, not quite half full, had freed itself from the cactus claws and was shining forth a wide-mouthed smile. Miguel smiled back a show of confidence intended for himself and turned, running down the alleys to avoid his little sister. His footsteps pounded heavy and hollow across the deserted valley, and became inaudible where he slowed at the turning of Millie's walk. At her porch he sat silently down and read his letter in the moonlight, wincing as he read. There was sincerity! There was conviction and convincingness! There were nicely turned literary illusions, an ill wind and the way to hell! Oh, fine. He abruptly turned another page and uncapped his pen.

Miss Delaney,

I plagiarized "The Snow Dove". I am going away.

MIGUEL

He ripped out the sheet and folded it irretrievably far beneath her door and ran again, back toward the mountain where the cliff dipped on the east side of the quarry. For half its height he scrambled at the same breathless pace over parched branches and splintery white pebbles which were dislodged by the thrust of his foot and slid away behind him with a shuffling noise. Then he slowed, the clutched book heaving on his chest, and gained the summit with more careful footing. He hung there a moment breathing, silhouetted in the tense half-crouch of an intended leap, edged thus along the white ridge for a step or two, and flung himself into the moon's smile.

He landed some eight feet down on two legs and one hand, picked himself up and repeated his leap for two less difficult distances, then sat on his notebook and, using it as a toboggan, slid the remaining steep and dusty thirty feet. He scarcely paused when his feet touched level ground, but retrieved the book and, catching a breathless laugh of exultation which the fresh valley wind flung in his face, rubbing an elbow scratch against his shirt, he skipped a few steps toward the Railton road, on to it toward the Railton track. Deceptively far in the clear night air, far too far to catch (but there would be another, there would be another), the west-coast headed Pocoho climbed out of Railton winking, and retreated noisily skyward up the dunes, a silver caterpillar, a flaming chariot, a wagon-load of stars.

XXV

Because the gold rush had passed Sintiempo by, disdainful of its dull and heavy treasure, the town had only one saloon, and that a relatively staid affair with leaded panes of bottle glass and dark-stained knotty pine panelling. Whatever domestic sort of frontier romance it had once possessed was negated now by a juke box dominating the single room—corpulent chrome and plexiglass which hiccupped a rainbow of revolving lights from the base to the selection board in evidence of perpetual indigestion. The nickelodion, fallen into long disuse, was relegated to a darker corner and the minor responsibility of bearing unwashed glasses. Tonight the place was empty but for Toad and a pair of acne-mottled younger boys in slightly self-conscious ranch dress, for women were seldom seen in the bar, and Sintiempo was not a drinking town.

"Putunickle in the buke jox!" one of the youths yelled loudly flipping a coin toward the counter and endeavouring to display as much drunkenness as possible. The bartender picked up the nickel and obediently walked to the

253

machine. He too was a young man, also pimply, with an excess of curly black hair, a ludicrously infantile pugged nose and a tendency to stammer. The sort whose friends no doubt, found him a trustworthy confidant, but unhappily not the man-of-the-world bartender one expects to absorb one's drunken grievances. Half the point of confiding to a stranger is that one must struggle to make him understand, or even listen. Whereas this one would have turned up pitying and limpid eyes; for all one knew, return the confidence and ask one home to dinner.

"Wh-what shall I p-play?" he asked inserting the coin uncertainly in the slot.

"You choosut Hoolihan!" yelled the young man who had thrown the nickel, and both of them broke into hysterical laughter when, after a moment of intestinal rumblings and metallic burps the machine began to bellow "The Mommy and Daddy Waltz".

> *I'd walk for miles,*
> *Cuhry or smiles,*
> *Fuh-hor muh mommy and daddy. . . .*

"You-who choose it, Hoolihan!" the young man screamed again, and flipping a dollar bill on the marble bartop he looped an arm around his companion's neck and the two of them stumbled out singing in ribald melancholy with the uncomfortable machine.

Oh, every day
I go an' pray
For mam- an' pahahappy.

"Shut it off, will you," Toad snapped and added when the juke box died, colour and sound, with a short electrical gasp, "and bring me another whisky."

"M-m-mister Ormerod," the young man said, "d-d-don't you think you ought to g-go home?" He spoke partly out of a natural veneration of moderation, partly from a sense of his role as bartender, partly because he could close the bar as soon as the last customer had gone.

"I'll be the judge of that," Karl said much more loudly than he felt like saying it, because he too had seen his part enacted many times and knew what attitudes a tough despair implied. The whisky was obediently brought.

And obediently drunk, in spite of a persisting sense that the stuff was made of rubbing alcohol and codfish oil. Karl had learned to drink on stolen creme de menthe from his mother's sideboard, and it was the only form of alcohol he really liked. There had been a time when the smell of beer reminded him of the taste of his own vomit, and he had spent what was, for him, a fair amount of effort at college learning to chugalug a pint. He held his liquor well, but he did not learn to like the taste of it. Still, a strong man cannot bathe a broken heart in creme de menthe, and even vodka seemed an ignobly bland antiseptic for such a wound. He therefore downed the unwatered whisky in one gulp and tried to sneak it past his palate.

It struck a match on his tonsils and burned both directions toward his nostrils and his stomach, an antidotal pain, worth more than drunkenness itself. He suddenly wanted to tell Millie that he didn't like liquor. He had, when he had drunk a lot, a vague conviction that having gone wrong for no apparent reason, their love would right itself at the sound of some irrelevancy. There were somewhere words he need only repeat; like the open sesame of Alibaba, and she would unfold with the old delight, the old expectancy. If only he could, like Alibaba, remember the words, or find them, or recognize them when they came to him.

"Millie," he would say, "I'll tell you something; I don't really like to drink. I only like the taste of creme de menthe, and I don't like that as much as peppermint." And she would listen with unaccountable solemnity rubbing a finger on her trouser knee as she had the morning he had described his father's bank. "Would you like to stay to lunch?" she would ask, and he would stay to lunch, would stay to dinner, stay to breakfast.

Karl watched a dribble of whisky descend the outside of his emptied glass, and shifted his gaze in impatient jerks from the dark octagonal window panes, to the mirror, to the bartender's fragile eyes, looking for the open sesame. Against the mirror at the back of the bar the squat thick whisky glasses were stacked in a pyramid upside down. As he watched they merged into a single unit and fell toward him and rolled back like a gracefully waved glass hand. He separated them into their proper immobility by counting them methodically, and there seemed then something diabolical in their very separateness. Seventeen of them on the lower row, sixteen on top of that, fifteen, fourteen, thirteen, twelve, on up to one, and the brash light glancing in the same arched rectangle on the curve of each.

"A shelf of glasses is all right," he would assure her seriously, "but glasses stacked are mathematics, there's the devil grinning out of them when you can't tell them apart." And she would tremble, her eyes would fill with tears, she would fling her arms about his waist and smash her nose against the pocket of his shirt. He made a fist against the pocket of his shirt. In his own eyes a jigger's worth of whisky-burning tears were poured.

"M-mister Ormerod," suggested the young man, who had been watching him all the while, "why d-d-don't you g-get a g-g-good night's rest."

Half-heartedly Toad grabbed up his glass and flung it at the bar. It hit the rail with an insignificant ping and bounced without breaking on the linoleum. The bartender sighed, walking to pick it up. Karl emptied his pocket on the table and went out. His sudden standing made him dizzy, and he leaned against a porch rail letting the tears spill down his cheeks and trying to set the swimming landscape into focus.

"Are you all right?" A dumpy woman with a plump bundle hesitated on the boardwalk.

"I have got," Karl said, "a pain in the crotch," and the woman hurried on clutching her package against her sagging breasts.

"It isn't catching," he called roughly after her retreating *derrière*.

He swung himself down off the porch and stumbled on through the otherwise deserted street. The hand of a giant pocket-watch above the jeweller's door jerked forward with a startling suddenness and a slightly dry sound.

"Millie," Toad said aloud, "it's ten to eleven. It's time for bed," and suddenly she was in the next shop window wearing a long shirt nightgown and a placard which boasted "Exceptional. $4.99". Exceptional. He flattened himself against the window with a hand against his groin and lifted an imploring lip to the mannequin. Then he wheeled away leaving a forehead, nose and chin of sweat on the glass, and walked ahead.

At the vacant lots the powdered ground gave way to irregular octagons of hard baked dirt, rather like the saloon's dark panes. Karl set his toes in the larger shapes for a little way, quite perfectly in spite of a sense that the ground was rolling to the left. "Do you remember", he would say, "that thing kids used to say at school—'Step on a line, you break your father's spine; step on a crack, you break your mother's back?' " And her face would light with recognition, she would jump up and run to the bookshelf to show him that it came from Shakespeare.

He held to a straight line toward Millie's house only until he could see the undulating outline of the shutters, firmly closed, offering nowhere the smallest sign of light or life. Somewhere at this moment she was lying there alone, her hair flung feathered in sharp relief against the whiteness of a pillow, one eyebrow so slightly higher arched than the other that only a lover would notice it; her small breast almost flat from the way she lay, so that the curve dipped to the side along her ribs and the perfect round of tender flesh rose waking to his touch. No, not now to his touch. He pressed his forehead into the stiff-haired bark. "God, Millie!" he said through gritted teeth against its roughness, against the stiff injustice, but even to his own ears the words were rather a whine than a cry. For Karl, who had never much wanted success at anything, his failure at unhappiness came with a force that spread to all his loved complacencies, like widening ripples from a rock dropped in a pond. He spun away from the tree and pounded his fist into the bark with all the force of his revolving body, and it is a matter of biological fact that if he had not died the next morning, the skin which broke on his knuckles against the dusty wood would have become seriously infected.

Still staggering slightly with the lightening pain and the force of his motion, he turned back to the road and headed for his shack at the quarry. He was a little disturbed to see, or seem to see, outlined against the violet reach of sky on the mountain top, a human figure like an insect, advancing sideways in a crouch. He watched it as far as the moon's edge, where it turned its back to him and flapped one arm like an insect wing, and he closed his eyes and looked again. The thing was gone.

"Good Christ," he said aloud.

Almost immediately he became aware of a childish chanting voice, of words more said than sung, but coming in such rolling soprano regularity that they seemed the background rhythm of a dream.

"Eres Paloma blanca

What made the sound particularly unreal was the fact that, although it savoured the foreign words with the lilt of Millie's voice, it pronounced them with the careful ease of a mother tongue.

An ancient Indian adobe, scarcely more now than a crumbling wall and a half of mud-embedded grass and bristly plants, blocked the singer from his view. It had once been a fairly large communal dwelling, and presumably because generations of cooking fires had baked its blocks to greater strength, the chimney still stood at its north-west corner. Toad drew silently to its shadow, and from there looked in to the girl at her pantomime. She had gathered a handful of sticky poppy stalks from which the petals had withered and left black powdery hearts, and she was trying, without breaking the rhythm of a ritual dance, to wedge them in a crevice between the blocks. . . .

Back and forward before the wall she stepped, swaying one direction and another with each repeated line of the song, and each time she passed the crevice she dipped the stems with the movement of her swaying, never compromising the cadence to force them into place. Where she stood the broken wall reached just above her knees, and over it muted moonlight polished the brown skin of her shoulders, the ebony of her flowing hair. The ruined flowers held at last, and then she bowed away from the wall, bending and bowing in a kind of private worship.

> *"Eres paloma blanca*
> *Como la nieve . . . ay-ay-ay-ay. . . ."*

She raised her arms and twirled about before her altar, letting the words fade into a high and steady monotone as she gathered speed. The lift of her arms stretched golden skin taut over bending ribs and raised the burnished nipples of her tiny breasts above the sunsuit bib. The slightest, softest raising of her moonlit flesh, like Millie Delaney lying on her back in a square of window sun. Karl caught his breath at the sudden tension in his groin.

Her hair fanned glistening in wheel about her
body as she twirled, so close to him once that it
grazed the chimney over which he watched, and
his hands clutched forward automatically, his
heart pounding to the base of his shivering
spine, to the pulsing of his injured knuckles.
The moon spun on her as she spun, lighting now
the vein behind her knee, the muscle of her bare
and slender thigh, now the hollow of her
armpits and the line of taut flesh leading to the
disc of darker flesh. His knees were weak, and
it was not his hands but his thighs could feel the
softness of flesh against his flesh. He would
have caught her but for the wall, and of the wall
he was only distantly aware, an unidentified
obstacle in a dream. Slowly he edged from the
shadow toward the lower rubble where the
stems were wedged, and he had almost reached
the corner when the girl stopped twirling
suddenly and tottering with dizziness fell
sitting against the chimney wall from which he
had just come. She pulled a lock of hair from her
shoulder and stuck it in her mouth with a
gesture so innocently and so impudently
childish that Karl's desire froze, and went limp,
and turned on him with disbelief and self-
disgust. Karl Ormerod, well-wisher, pacifist,

advocate of simplicity. He too sat down, and for some minutes they stayed on opposites side of the broken wall catching their breath, he with a painful attempt at total silence. Gradually this time he became aware of a Spanish voice, distant, nasal with anxiety.

" 'Riamariamaria, Miguelito!" the woman wailed from the village, and abandoning silence he stood and bolted toward the quarry, in a wide arc away from the Mexican town, not slowing until he had scrambled out of sight among the boulders. Then the two thoughts came to him together, as one two-sided thought, that he was going to be sick, and that there was a good chance he could coax a bottle of wine from one of the unmarried workmen in his barrack.

The Sun

XXVI

Karl Ormerod was killed on August first when he fell from a wagon on the way to the quarry, his head crushed by an oblique stroke of the wagon wheel which left his body so immaculately intact that even the workmen remarked it.

A load of dynamite, somewhat delayed by explosives regulations "for the duration", had arrived on Saturday, and because the quarry wagon was not there to receive them, had been delivered to the home of Foreman Pitz. There they might have remained until Monday if a tabby cat named Pangobon, dear to the heart of Mrs. Pitz, had not alarmed that lady by becoming entangled in the fuses of the box which had been opened for Mr. Pitz's inspection. Mrs. Pitz said that the dynamite would have to go, and was not assuaged by her husband's assurance that the fuses themselves were no more lethal than Mrs. Pitz's knitting yarn. She

266

kneaded her knitting with a lethal gesture, and Mr. Pitz snarled out toward the quarry.

At the barracks—a string of connected huts on concrete stilts, where the unmarried workmen lived—he rounded up such help as was to be found on a Sunday morning at nine o'clock: Karl and two other workmen in milder states of drunkenness. They took a two-horse wagon down the narrow and undulating cliff side path to the town, loaded the dynamite and took it back again. Karl's unsteadiness and his wild misjudgement of distance in the loading might have been as comical to the foreman as it was to the two Mexicans if Mr. Pitz had not instinctively felt that he must justify the unnecessary task with more than usual bad temper. Mr. Pitz took the reins and Karl sat on the front of the load while the other two weighted it at the outer corners of the back. A tarpaulin and a rope might have been more efficient, but the load was always steadied in this way, and the job was in fact particularly popular with the labourers because it gave rise to infinite variations, morbid and sexual and exceedingly funny, on the suppositions of danger in sitting on high explosives. Being drunk, the young and the old Mexicans enjoyed themselves more than usual over these inventions, while Mr. Pitz retained a surly silence and Toad, grasping the outer edge of each crate and leaning forward over the rump of the left-hand dray horse, seemed almost to sleep. At one of the many hairpin curves in the arduous, ill-kept climb, the front left wheel lurched over a deep rocky rut. Toad lost his balance and his hold on the crates, and his head as he fell forward struck the dray horse on the outer thigh, so that she in turn lurched forward with enough force to grind the wheel over the obstacle which was by that time in its path. At almost the same moment the reins checked her motion, and when the wagon came to rest its wheels were an innocent and equal distance from Toad's broken face, one on either side. From the workmen's view, he might have been sprawled for a rest with his head in the shade of the wagon bed.

He was not yet dead. His forearms raised slightly from the ground, and the fingers curled tensing the white muscles and the beautiful blue veins toward his elbow, but he did not precisely make a fist. The untouched eye and a corner of his mouth opened together with a mild, uncomprehending expression, and he said,

"Millie, I," before the sounds became a gurgle, and he lay silent then in exquisite strength from the shoulders down, so that it was not known in which of the next twenty minutes he died.

Mr. Pitz took one of the horses back to Sintiempo, and as he could not find the doctor, returned with Dr. Kregg, the dentist, rightly assuming that nothing would be needed but a medical signature on the death certificate. When they arrived the conscientious and now sobered workmen had already buried Toad Ormerod and marked the shallow mound with a green mesquite branch, which may have been an apology for being there at all instead of at the village mass, and were reloading a crate which had broken falling from the wagon bed. Dr. Kregg averred that a grave was adequate evidence of a death, and was not nearly so anxious to hear the details of the accident as Mr. Pitz, now no more surly than the Mexicans were now raucous, was to enumerate them. But when the foreman got to the dead man's last words, Dr. Kregg was impressed and rather touched, and it was with a feeling of some importance, and some urgency, that he strode back to town on foot while the others took the load on to the quarry.

Quite naturally, he did not go directly to Millie Delaney, and it seemed quite as natural that he did go to Mrs. Angleberger. She was after all as much of a mother as Millie had had for eleven years, and he was pleased to have some news for her which was at once startling and solemn. He had always been as much intimidated as impressed by the woman because of the extraordinary size of her teeth.

The Anglebergers had returned from church and, concurring in inarticulate monosyllables about the heat of the morning and of sabbath dress, had littered the house from the kitchen door to the bedroom with articles of superfluous apparel: a pink beflowered pillbox hat on the table, white gloves on the sink, a tie on the dining-room sideboard, a cowhide belt on the couch, damp shoes in the hall, a damp shirt on the seat of a chintz slipper chair. Finally Lena had shed her linen suit on the bed and shrugged into a square-shouldered cotton dressing-gown, and now, limp with the effort, she was wilting into the faded flowers of the sofa slip-cover. Duncan, shirtless, sat on the matching chair and distracted her from the church bulletin with an exposition of the vision which had come to him during Reverend Lemming's service. The discussion was in a fair way toward becoming a quarrel.

"You ever seen a smoker fumbling for his matches?" he demanded. "You ever seen Kep Hilton run out of lighter fluid? You tell me what a man like Kep Hilton wouldn't pay for a self-lighting cigarette."

Lena did not reply. A hole had frayed in the chequered elbow of her dressing-gown, and she was conscious of it with the slightest movement of her arm. She was conscious of it when she turned the page of the bulletin and read the words, "Is there a thing of which it is said, 'See, this is new'? It has been already, in the ages before us," which was the text of Neville Lemming's sermon. Reverend Lemming was not a man to baulk at Ecclesiastes, and in the context of his talk, the phrase had come to be a proof of the hereafter. But somehow all Lena could remember was that there had been a time when the dressing-gown seemed new. And it was not so long ago that the square padded shoulders, even squarer on her shoulders than they had been intended, had not seemed a daring espousal of radical chic. Through the ravelling her elbow thrust itself when she bent her arm, at once bony and wrinkled, at once flabby and hard, like a wattle on a stick, surely the most impudently ugly of the body's parts.

"What wouldn't he?" Duncan insisted. "All you got to have is a little slip of cardboard on the end, for strengthening, you see? And then there you got a little gob of phosphorus, and strip of sulphur on the package, like on a matchbox. Nothing simpler."

"Duncan," Lena said crossly, running a finger around her elbow on the frayed edge, "what's got into you this Sunday? You know we never, you know you don't believe in smoking."

"Then", Duncan continued, "you strike the cigarette on the side of the pack, so: and you puff on it before the flame goes out." He held his fingers in a victory V and puckered sucking at the air behind them.

Lena dug her elbow in her ribs to hide the bald patch and compressed her lips menacingly. "It has been already, in the ages before us," she said.

Duncan blinked and brought out the words he had been expecting to hear. "We could make a fortune," he prompted her.

"Well, Duncan Angleberger, is that what you've got to thinking about in church? Cigarettes? That's a sabbath picture."

"Crimea," Duncan protested, but he had not yet begun to invent statistics proving that cigarette consumption must be taken as an accepted fact, when the front door sounded and Dr. Kregg, waving aside Lena's apologies for the dressing-gown, entered formally below a deep furrow.

Dr. Kregg was a tall and, except for a weakness of chin which haunted him incessantly, a handsome man of about forty-five. In spite of his height he had never looked quite adult, and even now his greying temples were less distinguished than they might have been because of the original ashy blondness of his hair. He said that he would not sit down.

Briefly, with professional reserve, he repeated Joshua Pitz's story. Somewhere between Karl and Mrs. Angleberger the dead man's actual last word had been mislaid. It may have been that Mr. Pitz had not heard it, or forgotten it, or failed to make it articulate to Abel Kregg. It may have been that Dr. Kregg had not heard it, or forgotten it, or failed to make it articulate to Mrs. Angleberger. However it happened, Mrs. Angleberger heard, and thrilled with gooseflesh to the elbow hidden in her palm, that Karl

Ormerod's last word had been the name of Millie Delaney.

"I thought you might like to know," Dr. Kregg concluded with a solemnity which at once flattered Mrs. Angleberger and emphasized his devotion to duty, "that at the end, he was thinking of the girl."

Mrs. Angleberger thanked him ardently, with brimming eyes, and he took his departure. She released her elbow and rolled the church bulletin in a tight spiral from one corner. Duncan sat with his hands folded on the hump of his undershirt, staring at his stockinged toes. "Poor Millie Delaney," he said at last.

His words released a spring in Lena, and with a decisive gesture she flung the uncurling paper on the couch and unknotted her bathrobe sash. She strode just over the threshold into the hall and stepped into her shoes. Duncan, a little baffled, followed her to the bedroom and watched as she velveted her already rouged cheekbones with a carmine puff.

"Poor Millie Delaney," he said more loudly, rather resenting her frivolous activity and wishing to have an equal share in Millie's sorrow. "What will she do now?" Lena was painting the taut line of her lips, and did not reply. "It'll about do for her, I expect," he murmured.

Lena snapped the cap back smartly on the lipstick tube. "Duncan," she said, "you are a fool." While she dropped the robe to the floor and fought her way through the tube of linen skirt, he scratched at the thinness of his pate and repeated stubbornly, "Poor Millie Delaney, poor baby, tch."

"Duncan," Lena said with contemptuous volume fumbling at the twenty tiny buttons of her jacket, "supposing I were to leave you." Duncan was at a loss to grasp this sudden threat, and said only, "Lena?"

"Exactly!" she triumphantly shoved a button through its loop. "And supposing you were to think I left you because I didn't love you, and you were to close up the house and refuse to see a soul, or the light of day." Duncan backed up slightly and she whisked past him into the hall. "And supposing I were to die, and you were to find out that I died thinking of you, with your very name upon my lips."

Duncan's imagination would not follow her this far, but his stockinged feet followed the thump of her heels over the floor, to the living-room, to the dining-room, to the kitchen, where she snapped the band of her hat in place and shoved her fingers excitedly into her gloves. "How would you feel?" she demanded wheeling on him.

"I . . . I . . ." Duncan stuttered, having no idea what the next word was. "Come he left her then?" he asked instead.

"Whoo knows", Lena yodelled wringing the gloves smooth on her hands, "how we all misjudged him? Who knows how Millie did? Who knows how we all misunderstand these things?"

"What are you going to do?"

"Do? I," Lena swept open the kitchen door and drew herself up on the threshold with one hand stretched forth to the knob, "am going to bring Millie Delaney out."

July 31st. With care, she pencilled an X across the date, then tore the page from the calendar and crumpled it into the hearth, leaving August waiting on the pebbled wall. After that there seemed nothing to do.

Since her illness she had had to feed her restlessness with little tasks and non-existent urgencies, and tonight her restlessness seemed not of a greater intensity but of a different mould. Her hand played over the furniture, trying to awake again the sense of her possession; the needle point was harsh, and its harshness set her teeth on edge. She wanted to rub the too soft finger-tips on something hard and cool, but the marble table top brought no relief.

For several hours now her very skin had felt of a different stuff, as if she had been stripped of some protective covering; when she leaned to the calendar her breast brushed against the bookcase edge, and the skin ached with a subtle staying pain.

For several hours now she had felt from throat to stomach a vague constriction and a hollowness, not identifiable, and yet in some way familiar. She had thought that it must be hunger, but whatever she ate lay heavy, and the dull hollowness increased.

Catch-images of her memory which had for a month been nothing to her but the source of a great inertia played with her mind at the end of puppet strings, a helplessness toward hatred; and for moments she was alternately obsessed with the stupidity of the prescribed curriculum, with the stupidity of Doreen Sammon, with her father's assumption of his own superiority, with Sintiempo's uncomprehending acquiescence, with the sound of her mother's measured voice saying, "It doesn't matter so much what you do in life, Millie, as long as you are nice." She wondered if she had ever been nice, excepting in the reflection of some moted eye.

She paced thus through the house until twelve o'clock, in a depression that had no relief because it had no direction, and at last, indecisively, she went to bed. She snapped the dining-room light once on and off—the moon was there—and wandered upstairs, bathed and undressed at a pace that would have been leisurely if it had not been tense, and stretched out flushed and steaming in Geegee's sheets. The sheets grated against her skin. The heaviness spread to her back and settled dully at the base of her spine, so that she twisted and tangled herself in her gown, and could nowhere find a position that did not suffocate her with her own swollen weight. Her mind fingered idly the objects of her past; their needle point was harsh, and the hard cool stuff of her seclusion brought no relief. If for a brief space she rested, she thought, there, now I am going to sleep, and was awake again.

When she slept at last it seemed the fraction of a second before she awakened, and wondered quietly where the baby was. She didn't remember having seen him for several days. She rose and descended the twilight-coloured stairs, wandering through the house toward the living-room, but losing her way. The stairs led into the dining-room, not toward the book-shelved walls as before, and when she snapped the light off the shutter remained as still and solid as before. She crossed what should have been the right sill, and was in the kitchen; the kitchen door led to another flight of stairs, and when she reached the bottom of these she was in the master bedroom. This led back into the kitchen, the kitchen into her own small room from which there was no exit but the door through which she had come. She tried the window, but it was barred. She opened the clothes closet, and her baby was there, crawling head down under the spindly legs of a bassinet. Without lifting his head, he gave a little cry of delight and crawled forward reaching for her feet. She remembered later with great clarity his delighted cry of recognition. She leaned forward extending both index fingers, and these he grasped, the right one with a wrinkled hand on which there were, she was not sure how many, but too many fingers. His face when he lifted it was the face of an apple-cheeked old man, curiously pockmarked, curiously wrinkled, stern; like the face of a baby in a medieval painting. She was not startled, but profoundly saddened by his deformity.

"Hello. Where have you been?" she asked, and he answered obediently, "Down stairs to see the fights." "Well, that's all right," she said, trying to hide her anxiety, "but next time you want to go I wish you'd tell me, and I'll go with you. I worry when I can't find you." He said very sweetly that he was sorry, and that he would not go without her again, and she picked him up and laid him in the bassinet. He could not have been more than a few weeks old. Under his sweet weight she felt again in a great slow wave, not horror, but sad love for his grotesqueness. She wanted desperately not to let him know.

Whether this dream came early in the night or in the morning toward her waking, Millie never knew. She had seemed to fall straight from her sleeplessness into it, and yet she woke wrapped in a deep fog of it, silently crying for the sadness of it, even when she knew that it was not real. She could not swallow, and the heaviness in her spine had become a blunt pain which, when she stirred, flowed through the muscles of her thighs and up her neck, binding her head. The dull emptiness of her stomach had spread itself through all her body, and the pressure, too defined, too familiar now to remain unidentified, weighted itself toward the hollow of her groin. And yet for perhaps five minutes she lay fighting morning, fighting consciousness, fighting the knowledge of her trickling blood.

It was almost noon by the time she breakfasted. She drank something, and ate something, she could not have said what. She chewed, she swallowed, in all likelihood she digested. She paced about in sandals on the kitchen linoleum. Knowing her depression of the night before imposed, and therefore partially unreal, she should have been free to reason with it now, to force the elements of her life back into the perspective she had seen a month ago, in which they were equal, and equally devoid of meaning. Had she not always and only wanted freedom? Had she ever been able to want the child as anything but an image of her own withdrawal? What had after all so obsessed her in the prospect of her bastard but a sense of the just bizarre? Had she not accepted it only, in spite, to infect the whole unrealizing ugliness with something it would not recognize as itself? To defy an amoeba of unrefined carnality, and to make of it a being of unalloyed reason. Dully to fear, listlessly to accept, bitterly to desire, simply to lose . . . she had the freedom that had been her only wish. But from that freedom her self stretched now before her, seven counties, four states, two countries of trackless sand.

"I am so glad," she said with finality aloud. But when she tried to make her shopping list, she couldn't even bring herself to write the

name of her need. She had known she could
keep the child's existence to herself, and yet she
was now ashamed to publish its non-existence,
as if all Sintiempo had guessed her pregnancy,
and would wonderingly whisper, "Millie
Delaney isn't having a baby after all". And
though she had not thought of Miguel in any
context from the end of June but snatches of his
poem treading through her thoughts, she could
not bring herself to inflict embarrassment on
him, or to make him the source, the bearer of
her shame.

"Absorbent cotton," she scribbled, and
ashamed of her weakness she hurried to shove
it out of sight beneath the door. She picked up
the folded paper lying there.

Miss Delaney,
I plagiarized "The Snow Dove". I am going
away.
MIGUEL

She fingered the note and folded it in her
pocket. She wondered where he had learned the
cumbersome legal term. For several moments
she stood running her fingers through a lock of
lifeless hair that fell across her forehead,

283

holding the fingers still and revolving her head toward and away from them. I haven't any way to get food, she thought.

And suddenly she could not separate Miguel from the girl she had believed she carried, from the gentle deformed creature of her dream. Her waking, her seeping blood, this cryptic note were losses of things she had not owned. And yet not losses of the things themselves; not of the girl, but of a mind that could not do otherwise than understand; not of the baby but of the precious secret of his deformity; not of Miguel but of the hopeful lie she had believed of him. They retreated from her substanceless as shadows, indifferent as symbols, expressionless as the old woman had been in death.

"I don't know them," she said in protest, and said then in repentance, "I don't know them." She closed her eyes, and with an effort as confused and nebulous as her thoughts she tried to remember what she had wanted of her life, to discover a pattern she had somewhere lost. But only, in swift shadow show on her eyelids, she saw her life narrowing from its hope of an ever-higher heaven to Sintiempo's mountain closure, from Sintiempo to her shuttered house. She covered her eyes as if to retreat once further still. "Let . . ." she whispered, by which she meant, let me be free of the world. But the throbbing in her thighs scattered the thought before it formed. She steadied herself on the edge of the sink, but withdrew her hand sharply from the buttery blade of her mother's butcher knife.

I do not know, she suddenly thought, what people are thinking before they kill themselves. I don't know what they feel.

She picked up the knife and aimed it toward herself first at her stomach, then adjusting it higher toward her heart. Even in the artificial light the edge shone yellow. She must have used it to butter her bread.

She turned it curiously over in her hand and moved it sharply, but not far, toward the swelling of her breast. Her gesture startled her, and without trying to she imagined the point plunged further forward, imagined something altogether unlike the heaviness in her womb— cold, shooting, sharp—and in the tone of a child who has been given an unreasonable command she cried, "I *will* not". An impulse she had thought altogether dead burst from her as if with the force of long restraint, and she formed the words, inaudibly again, "I will not die, I will not. . . ."

She relaxed her hand and the blade dropped swinging. She watched the melted butter roll to the point and drip once on the floor. She gripped it again and revolved her fist, watching the knife turn away from her, conscious of its innocence and its solidity, and that it had nothing to do with her. She slid it into the sink, and it lay rocking on its handle with a gentle wooden sound. She took out again Miguel's confession, and read it over smiling at the legal word.

Then the last hope is gone, she said to herself, but her mind stood looking on at her disappointment; something detached from disappointment, repulsion, loneliness itself; asking her reasonably what, after all, had constituted hope, and why she expressed herself so feebly.

She crossed into the living-room, concentrating on nothing but the sound of her sandals over the carpet, and played her hands across her books. In the half-dark she could recognize *The Republic* by a raised oval where its title would be; *Paradise Lost* by the indentation of Milton's name in script; *Great*

Expectations by the texture of its spine, smooth to the finger-tip, but giving forth a slight zipping sound from a finger-nail across the grain. She pressed her fingers in the grooves between them until their substance became real to her, letting their touch recall their phrases: ". . . do you think that such men would have seen anything of themselves or of each other except the shadows. . . ?"

When she reached the mirror she placed her fingers on the glass and traced there the flat outline of her face, still thinner than it had been before, sharp in the eyes and jaw; a schoolteacher's face. She ran her fingers in the same oval outline on her skin and bit her index finger, feeling separately the pressure on skin and nail and tooth. She could just make out in the darkness behind her the shape of the empty rocking chair. She wheeled and bent before it, folding her arms on the leather seat and rocking her head in the crook of her elbow. The chair responded with its monotonous, identifying whine. "Catch your death on the floor, Millie; all work and no play; come over into the light, you'll ruin your eyes." She grasped the chair to still it as, for the first time, the immensity of Geegee's loneliness, and her death, struck home to her.

She thought of her own vague pretence with the kitchen knife, of the extremes of hope and suffering that had cancelled themselves toward that grotesque cliche; of how deeply one must understand to understand, "A stitch in time; catch your death on the floor; the last hope is gone."

She rocked again, and the chair's bleak rhythm pulsed through her like new blood. Her thoughts flowed with the sound, and with her thoughts, the rich relief of guilt. She pressed her weight against the wood and let its own weight press her back, rocking, rocking herself into a corporeality she had disdained to share. She had scorned her father's self-monument in stone, asking for herself some more imperishable shrine. She had built her life on a child's vision of the sky, and denying the stones she stumbled on, convinced herself that falling was a kind of flight. She had hated Sintiempo's self-approbation, and called her hatred virtue; had discovered the expanse of her own littleness, and called it knowledge. Not that she had been wrong. Not that their righteous scratching would leave its trace, but that seeing her task in its true proportion, she had refused responsibility, had denied that duty was to accept the infinitesimal task, to devote the infinity of a soul to it, and not despair. She had wound her littleness into a tighter, self-constricting coil, until at the moment of its breaking she acknowledged after all her need. Between the decision and the act is the impulse ... I will not die, I will not. The mind despairs in abstracts, but the hand and the knife play out their affairs in time and space. The most that the mind can say is, life is not worth anything, and nothing is not the impetus to death. August was waiting on the calendar.

She thought of Socrates, knowing behind his coquetry, his ignorance; she thought of Lucretius, despairing before the splutter and the slime; she thought of St. Augustine, posing questions of a god whose answers he could only guess. She thought of them in the passionate and difficult years of setting their monumental insignificance to words. She thought of the sound of chalk on slate, of the smell of new October shoe-leather, of the belly of Bombo of the Congo on the glossy page.

She rose a little stiffly and stilled the chair. At the door she splayed a hand on the dark pebbled paper, closing her eyes against the wrist, and, longingly, "Oh, my cave," she said.

In the kitchen the knife had stopped rocking on its white marble bed, and the latch gave easily, almost without sound.

June and August are the same in the desert but for a fiercer blinding at the summer's end, and Sintiempo was without change. The sun struck out at her unaccustomed eyes, ricocheted from metal rooves and broken glass, rose steaming from the trees and flung at her a vast mirage of brandished swords and shields aloft and flower vendors turning in the breeze: Athens, and Chaos, and Chelsea. Toward her in the distance strode a woman with flowers in her hair, stooped in the centre of the shimmering glass, rose and resumed her stride: Andromache *en route* to the wall of Troy.

Mrs. Angleberger walked quickly, squinting toward Millie's house as if it might offer some prophetic sign of welcome. When she got to the vacant lots, however, she had to keep her eyes on the ground for fear of catching a heel in the cracks. She could not compromise her haste to the dust that stirred around her shoes and sifted through the ventilation holes of the plastic mesh.

She had the ability to concentrate on her footing without being distracted by the garish bits of glass, but when she noticed a length of darning cotton stretched across her path, she drew abruptly up and squarely stooped to it. The heavy thread, a little dusty, but unknotted and a good yard long, zigzagged across the zigzag cracks and ended under the shaded foot of a prickly pear. She tugged on it, and withdrew the dried shell of a sequiny desert beetle. It powdered in her fingers.

"*That's* a saving," Mrs. Angleberger said to herself with satisfaction, and rising quickly she resumed her urgent stride toward Millie's house, skeining the cotton on her fingers and

tucking it, for safe keeping, in the bosom of her
jacket.